The Broken Queen

Sherry Ficklin

Clean Teen Publishing

Broken Queen

Printed in the United States of America

Clean Teen Publishing
www.CleanTeenPublishing.com

Summary: Desperate and willing to sacrifice anything—and anyone—to her gambit, Elizabeth must make the final choice between the destiny that was promised to her and one man she might truly love.

ISBN: 978-1-63422-392-8 (paperback)
ISBN: 978-1-63422-393-5 (e-book)
Cover Design by: Marya Heidel
Typography by: Courtney Spencer
Editing by: Cynthia Shepp

YOUNG ADULT FICTION / Historical / Europe
YOUNG ADULT FICTION / Royalty
YOUNG ADULT FICTION / Romance / Historical

YA

content disclosure

For more information about our content disclosure, please utilize the QR code above with your smartphone or visit us at

www.cleanteenpublishing.com.

Prologue

Anna's coronation is like no event I've ever witnessed. Inside the grand Assumption Cathedral of Moscow, she kneels at the altar, her simple gold-brocade gown modestly arranged around her. Fashioned in the German style, her raven-black hair is plaited on either side of her round face. The former Duchess of Courtland waits to be elevated to the empress of Russia—a title that should have been mine. By birth and by right, the position had been offered to me, but with acceptance came terrible conditions—conditions that would have made me an empress in title only, leaving the real power in the hands of the Supreme Council. I'd refused such mockery, but Anna had accepted without hesitation. Anna Ivonivich, daughter of my father's addled brother, now sits on the throne that should rightfully be mine. But even as I watch, knowing I should be enraged by the display, the only emotion I can muster is a bone-deep terror.

Anna is surrounded by the members of the

Supreme Council, the men gathered like wolves waiting to attack. Not only are the lords and ladies of the great houses in attendance, but also commoners as well, which is a tradition my father started long ago. At my back, General Sergei Saltykov stands, his hand never far from the pommel of his blade. He's my friend, advisor, lover, and most devout protector, and the dread I feel is an emotion he no doubt shares. Without even looking back, I'm confident he's scanning the room with his piercing green eyes, on high alert for any rumblings of danger.

The crown is on Anna's head before the ink on the council's letter of conditions has even had time to dry. The council moved swiftly for fear I'd return from St. Petersburg with an army at my back. But my grief from losing Peter had been too fresh. I'd been numb, paralyzed almost, and incapable of doing anything quickly. Instead, I traveled here to watch the passing of my father's throne once again, with no one but Sergei to accompany me, and only because the empress demanded I come.

At least Peter was a good man who tried to be a good king. That alone had earned him my support. But with him gone…

Resolutely, I shake away the memories of him, of the times—far too few—we'd shared.

One would think I'd be used to it by now, but the sight of the archbishop placing my father's crown upon Anna's head chills me to the core. It's all I can do to keep my expression neutral. If I allow the encroaching fear beating within my chest to leave its proof upon my face, it will mark me as easy prey.

There can only be two reasons why I was summoned to witness the crowning ceremony. Either the council wants me to officially support Anna—and renounce my claim—or they want to declare me a traitor, then exile me to Siberia or send me to my death at the gallows. If it's the latter, Sergei has a plan with the horses already saddled and waiting for our daring escape. We'll flee to France, if we must, and seek shelter there. The very idea of it, leaving Russia to Anna and the council, twists my stomach. I might as well be signing my own nation's death sentence, forsaking the land my ancestors built from the bones of squabbling knights and warring peasants.

Crowned, Anna turns, scepter in hand, and addresses the assembly in a booming voice.

"My people, you have a new empress this day."

The crowd cheers wildly, even as the council members exchange nervous glances. It's unusual for a monarch to speak inside the chapel, even more so for them to address the assembly so informally.

"And yet..." she continues. "There are those among you who seek to bind me. Who seek to rule this great nation in secret."

The cheers turn to boos, the attendees becoming riotous. Eyes widening, I can do nothing but gape as

I begin to understand her plan.

Stepping forward, she speaks louder. "What would you prefer, my people? That your true empress bow to the whims of these lesser men? Or that I, chosen and anointed by God himself, should lead this nation?"

They shout their approval for the second choice. I watch the growing chaos, my bones filling with dread.

"What is she doing?" Sergei whispers, suddenly right beside me. Lifting me to my feet, he drags me backward until we are against the wall.

"I do not know," I say, scanning the crowd. Finally, I find the faces of the men responsible. Their confusion and fear echo my own.

Raising a plump hand, Anna points to them. "These men have forced me to sign away my ruling powers. Do you think I should obey?"

The cheering becomes chanting.

"Tear it up. Tear it up. Tear it up," the mob demands.

Count Bestuzhev approaches Anna, scroll in hand. Dramatically, she yanks it away, then holds it over a nearby candle until it bursts into flames. The crowd cheers.

"Guards, seize these men," she orders.

They try to flee, but it's too late. The majority of the council members are rounded up, shackled, and forced to their knees before the new empress, only a few managing to escape in the commotion. Anna's round cheeks are flushed, her lips curled into a thin, cruel smirk.

"And what shall their punishment be?" she demands of the crowd, continuing the obscene spectacle.

"She wouldn't," Sergei says, his eyes wide with surprise.

Of course she would. Her own father had been denied the throne because his mind was so twisted and rotted no one dared entrust him with it. That he'd produced offspring at all was a crime against nature itself.

Now, here stands his daughter, a lifetime's worth of rage flowing from her like an ocean. And we are all going to drown in it.

"We need to get you out of here," Sergei demands, ushering me toward the door.

Before we can make it through the horde, Count Bestuzhev blocks our escape.

"Do not flee. The empress would speak with her cousin," he orders firmly.

I cannot disobey. Whatever fate Anna has in store for me, there is no escaping it now. I can only nod, placing a hand on Sergei's arm to keep him from slashing our way out. Whatever happens now, he, at least, will have the chance to run. I'll make sure of it.

Anna continues playing to the crowd, speaking

now to the men at her feet.

"The people have spoken. This council is abolished. And you, the architects of that pitiful document, are to meet your fates at the block!"

All around us, people begin to scream. Some in approval; others in sheer disbelief. The guards yank the men to their feet, shoving them out of the church in a rough line. Anna takes her time following, cutting a noble path through the crowds of people, who cheer and scream for justice.

We trail after her. The council leaders are paraded down the streets of Moscow, straight to the block, while still in their finery. As they pass, spectators throw rocks at them, the entire city demanding their blood.

The guards line them up one by one in the square. While a part of me wants to turn away, to jump on a horse and flee for my life, I cannot. These men betrayed not only Anna, but also me, Peter, and the entire country. And I can't help but be glad that if I do lose my head this day, I'll live long enough to watch them lose theirs first.

Anna comes to my side, wrapping an arm through mine. I tremble at the touch. She's smiling, not in joy but in malice, and it radiates from her like heat from a fire.

"I wanted you to see, dear cousin. A gift to you—to us both."

At a wave of her hand, the first ax falls, severing

Count Ostermann's head from his neck. Blood sprays, flowing down the wooden platform as the executioner moves from one man to the next, his blade so dull by the end he has to strike his final victim three times before making it clean through. With each head that rolls, Anna squeezes me harder. Her face is twisted in excitement. It is not the blood, but the pleasure she takes in it that revolts me, turning my stomach until I pitch forward and vomit.

She releases me quickly, smoothing her hands down her gown to check I haven't soiled her.

"A weak stomach, cousin? Your father would be disappointed," she chastises. "I'd have thought you'd enjoy seeing these heathens receive their fates."

Wiping my mouth with the back of my hand, I answer carefully. "It's not that, Your Highness. I haven't eaten yet today."

Suspiciously, she glares at me. "You're not with child, are you?"

"No," I assure her. "That would not be possible."

She laughs, and it only nauseates me further. "Still a maid, are you? Well, I suppose one can't believe every rumor. Come, let's go enjoy the feast. I'm sure some meat and wine will settle you."

Still quaking, I straighten my back and follow her procession to the palace, where a grand meal has been laid out. One of her guards leads me to a chamber where a gown has been laid out for me. Adorned with no lace or finery, it's only a simple, brown cotton dress like what a servant might wear. She's making a point. I am no one now. She is my master, and I am but a lowly servant.

Disposing of my soiled gown, I change slowly with no ladies to attend me. Pulling the pearl pins from my hair, I arrange it into two braids, weaving them around the back of my head. I wash my face, scrubbing away the carefully applied rouge and eye coal. Perhaps if I look the part she wants me to play, I might leave this place with my neck intact.

Quietly slipping into the feast, I sit to the left of the empress, amid three empty chairs. Sergei's gaze finds me through the crowd. Clearly relieved, he exhales deeply, then takes up a position near the door.

"What will you do with the rest of the council?" I ask Anna after she has enjoyed several glasses of wine.

"I haven't decided. They will be hunted down, obviously, like the dogs they are, then brought here for judgment. The real question is, cousin, what shall I do with *you*?"

The threat in her voice is plain. I cannot stop the wave of fear that washes over me, making me shudder. Looking down at my plate, I clear my throat.

"I am yours to command, Your Highness."

I feel her eyes on me for a long moment before she leans over, whispering in my ear.

"You have witnessed the price of betraying your queen. So long as you keep my favor, you will keep your head. Do you understand?"

"I do. Thank you for your mercy, Empress."

Standing, she lifts her glass, "Gentleman, please join me in a toast to my dear cousin Elisabeth, Princess of Russia. She will be returning to St. Petersburg to maintain my palace until my return."

The table goes quiet, but they hesitantly lift their glasses, everyone clearly wondering if her words are some sort of trap or test.

"To Princess Elizabeth," they finally mutter.

I stand, raising my own glass. "To our esteemed empress, long may she reign."

There is more enthusiasm this time, and Anna blushes before returning to her chair.

The feast continues around us, but I lock my eyes on Sergei, who stands stoically by the door. He nods once, but he does not relax. I doubt he will breathe again until we are free of this place.

The servants bring out more trays, covered in silver domes. As they set them on the table, conversations resume, casual, if tense.

Until the moment when the lids of the dishes are removed, displaying three severed heads on silver platters.

My stomach revolts again, but Anna claps, laughing.

"One last meal with our fallen council," she

orders, raising a glass once more.

I shift toward her. "Empress, forgive me, but my stomach has soured again. I fear I should take my leave."

Apparently, I'm not the only one who feels it. Disgust visibly crashes over the room as ladies swoon, and men run for the door.

"Go then, cousin. I do not want to see your face in Moscow again—not unless it's by my order," she demands.

After I agree, I force myself to walk—not run—to the door where Sergei waits. He bows, then takes his leave behind me.

Only once we are outside do I dare draw breath again, the odor of meat and death clinging to me.

"Are you all right?" he asks, offering me a steadying hand.

"We must go. Now."

"The horses are already prepared."

"Then let's escape this terrible place before our empress changes her mind."

Spring 1740

The halls of the Winter Palace are alive again after another long winter. Maids arrange fresh flowers in vases, carpets are swept, and the windows are thrown wide to let the fresh morning breeze flow through the corridors. The scent of hot tea and honey biscuits draw me from my bed, and I sit up, tossing my heavy woolen blankets aside.

Lady Lia is already bustling about my room, selecting my gown for the day. Older than me by some margin, she has broad shoulders, her dark hair showing the first strands of true silver as she stands with her sloping nose in the air.

"Did you sleep well, Your Grace?" she asks pointedly.

"I did, mostly thanks to your tonic."

"Has it eased the dreams, then?"

The dreams. Terrors of the night. They are mostly the same each time, only the faces changing. I'm trapped in the palace, with an army breaking down every door. I run, searching for my loved ones, hoping to protect them, to usher them to safety. When I throw open the door to the royal chamber, I find them dead on the floor, their heads some distance away. Sometimes, it's my father and my sister. Other times, it's Peter. Recently, though, it's someone else, the one person I've managed not to lose...*yet*.

Sergei.

Beaten and bloody, he has a sword pierced through his chest even as his lifeless green eyes seem to stare right at me.

I shake myself from the gruesome memory.

"You need new gowns," Lady Lia says, clicking

her tongue. Her French accent is thick, though her Russian is impeccable. Even now, I can scarcely believe she was born in the body of a man, for she is so thoroughly a woman. Clever and cunning, she's also tender and kind. Perhaps that's why the French king added her to his secret network of spies in the first place. Her presence is soothing, but her counsel is always sharp.

She's trying to distract me from my thoughts, and it's most welcome. I often doubt anyone can truly understand how I feel—forced into in a life, a lie, that I am somehow something other than I know I am—but she comes closest. She alone appreciates the pain of being trapped in the flesh of something one was never meant to be.

Groaning, I still flash her a smile. I have dozens of dresses, though Lia insists I change at least twice a day, as is custom in most of the European courts. By herself, I imagine she could keep the palace seamstresses busy for the next hundred or so years.

"What I need is for my cousin to raise the stipend she sends me to maintain the palace," I correct. "Of course, that's difficult to do when she's bleeding the coffers dry with her senseless frivolities."

"I heard she bought a ship full of exotic animals for her personal menagerie only last month."

I don't doubt it. Empress Anna, my cousin and the daughter of my addled uncle Ivan, has been on the throne only a few years, yet she has already nearly bled our once-prosperous nation dry.

Despite initially signing away all her rights as powers monarch in the same contract the Supreme Council had once offered me—an offer I'd vehemently refused—she has since filled every available court position with her German sycophants. None have any care when it comes to spending. She simply hasn't the forethought to care, but they must have other motives. A weak Russia is a target for the hungry German king, who presses at our borders while our troops are engaged to the east. They keep the empress well distracted with food, wine, and games while our nation slips between her fat fingers.

If I weren't so disgusted by her, I might admire her for the sheer defiance of it all. In truth, her ruthlessness comes as no surprise to me. I'd tried to warn them, after all, that the former Duchess of Courtland was not to be trusted. Once she secured the crown, anyone on the council who'd forced her to sign the document limiting her powers had been rounded up and either exiled or executed. A few had survived—either by fleeing or being forced to accept lesser positions in her court. Prince Golitsyn himself had been reduced to serving as her court jester before Anna had married him off to the most unattractive slave she could find. I'm told the empress had an ice palace erected for their wedding night, then sent them into it with no clothing, telling him to either find warmth in his new bride or freeze to death.

Then the Supreme Council had been disbanded in favor of her new Secret Office of Investigations, which has already seen a hundred souls swing at the gallows for speaking against her.

"The way she spends money on her amusements, it's a wonder she has anything to send at all," Lia says, holding one of the crimson brocade gowns out to me.

I nod. "So she does, by breaking the backs of the landlords and serfs alike. But at least her amusements keep her far away from us. Speaking of amusements, is everything in place for tonight's celebration?"

"It is. Though I doubt Sergei's name-day feast will come as much of a surprise to him. I doubt anything happens within these walls of which he is not aware."

My grin widens. Sergei is far too intelligent to surprise, but he is also wise enough to pretend, even if only for my sake. While I'm sure he'd prefer a more private celebration of his name day, it's been far too long since I've heard the sounds of laughter echoing through these halls. Through some careful planning of my own, I've saved enough for the occasional entertainment. As much as this feast is for Sergei, it's for the people as well, a small respite from the oppressive restrictions they've been struggling beneath since Anna was crowned.

Another opportunity for me to remind them who genuinely cares for and looks after them.

Truthfully, Anna has been quite generous, publicly at least. She allows me to stay in St. Petersburg, far from the Royal Court in Moscow, and I am the mistress of the palace. It has become *le petit royal*, as Lia calls it. Nobles come, seeking refuge or assistance, and I provide it as I see fit. Prince Vasily, who once was an ally, but who did not support me after Peter's death, sends plenty of funds directly to me in exchange for my keeping much of his family under my care, including his brother, Lukitch, who barely escaped the gallows himself.

I write to Anna once a week, apprising her of conditions here and accounting for the funds she sends. If she reads my letters, I do not know. She does not respond unless she requires something—which isn't often at all.

"At least the royal guard is flourishing again," I remark as Lia helps me into my corset and gown. "After Menshikov and his ilk nearly set us against half of Europe."

Lia snorts. "It's easy to maintain the troops when you're forcing them into service at ever-younger ages while lengthening the time they are required to stay."

"I have not heard complaints from the soldiers here. They seem happy enough to serve," I say with a frown, wondering if their fear of Anna has prevented them from being honest about their situations.

"Because they are here, serving you. There is honor in that, and you care for them so well. I believe you are godmother to half the children born to the regiment."

I consider her words, knowing there is not much I can do outside my limited reach. "The armies of Russia deserve better. They are our sword and shield, after all. But I can only do so much."

"I know you do what you can," Lia soothes, drawing a brush through my hair. "And so do they. I do think the former council must be rolling over in their graves at what the empress has done to the country."

"Would that I could feel some pity for them," I say, smirking. "Alas, I cannot. They plotted against Peter—and me—before his body was even cold. If the crown had fallen to me, I cannot say I would have done any differently. Her strategy on that count was nothing short of ruthless genius."

"You were still grieving Peter," Lia murmurs, laying a comforting hand on my shoulder. "It's a miracle you were thinking clearly at all."

Peter. After all this time, it still hurts to think about him. Sometimes, I wake up thinking I've heard the sound of his voice or felt the touch of his hand. Losing him changed me in ways I have yet to come to grips with. All I know is there is a pain within me that nothing seems to heal. Even Sergei—

my handsome, loyal general—can't fully quench the sorrow, though he tries.

"Grief cannot be an excuse for weakness. My father taught me that much."

"Anger can be managed, perhaps. But love and sadness? They come at their own time and are forces that cannot be denied, even by the most levelheaded person."

"Yet, denied they must be. A ruler cannot afford such blindness, even temporarily."

She smiles. "Well, we cannot change the past, only learn from it. I doubt you will ever find yourself in such a position again, but if you should, you will be even stronger because of it."

When she tightens the laces of my bodice, the air is pushed roughly from my lungs.

"Not so tight," I say with a groan. "But yes, I believe you are right. However, you must be careful with your words. We cannot give Anna any reason to doubt my loyalty. Even now, her secret army patrols the streets, searching for any who whisper against the empress so she might have one more body to torture for her own amusement."

"The maids say she keeps a gun beside her bed so she can shoot at people when they wake her."

I shrug. "I wouldn't doubt it. There is a reason Ivan and his children were not meant to inherit the throne. They were addled and twisted in the mind, the lot of them."

And I tried to warn the council of that fact, though my message fell upon deaf ears. They imagined the humble, widowed Anna would be easy to control. What threat could she pose? They were gravely mistaken on that count. No sooner had they placed the crown upon her head, then she had sliced off theirs.

"They conspired against not just you and Anna, but also the crown itself," she reminds me. "Would your father have done any differently?"

"No," I admit. "Treachery comes at a high price in Russia."

"And they paid for it with their lives."

I can only nod.

Once dressed, I eat quickly and head to my offices.

Sergei is already waiting there, and he bows when I enter. "Princess Elizabeth, I hope you slept well."

The one small kindness Anna allowed me, in exchange for my support, was to grant the return of my title. In truth, she only wanted to appear benevolent in hopes of gaining the support of those who still valued the Romanov name. She imagined herself quite clever because of it. I think it was one of her first and greatest blunders. Although it is a shallow title, with no real power behind it, it is a brick upon which I have been slowly, carefully building allies.

Swallowing, I avert my eyes as I lie. "Quite well, thank you."

"No more nightmares?" he asks.

When I glance at him, he has one eyebrow raised in doubt as he closes the door.

I sigh heavily. "I should not have burdened you with that."

Crossing the room, he gently takes my hand. His skin is warm against mine, comforting and stifling at the same time. "It's no burden, Lizzy. I worry for you is all. Please don't pull away from me now. Let me help you."

Inside me, the pain rolls like a tide against the shore, crashing against my ribs. If I give in, it will take me under completely. I will drown in my own grief. With great effort, I force it down, silencing it with a fragile dam of sheer will. For only a moment, I let Sergei hold me, allowing his warmth to drive the chill from my bones. He is my only refuge in this tempest-tossed existence, but I must be careful. The one thing I know he longs for above all else is something I simply cannot give him. And that, coupled with the fact Anna has spies everywhere, just waiting for me to make a single misstep, would be my downfall. If she discovers I care for Sergei in any true way, there's no doubt she'd have him exiled or worse.

"I am all right," I reassure him. "At least, I will be once we check on the progress of the new canal."

Opting not to press me further, Sergei releases me with a sigh, then takes a seat across from me with the desk between us. "I am surprised Anna agreed to continue building here in St. Petersburg, especially with her own court so far removed."

Frowning, I shuffle through the pages on my desk. "I doubt it was Anna who ordered the construction to proceed. More likely, it was Duke Byron."

"He is the Duke of Courtland, correct? Isn't his wife Anna's lady-in-waiting?"

I nod. "She is. However, that has not prevented Anna from taking the duke as her lover and personal pet. I'm told she has little care for anything of politics, so she leaves those matters to him to decide."

"Oh? Has she set Bestuzhev aside so soon?"

"Rumor has it she has. Supposedly, she is now surrounding herself with a new group of Germans. They are counseling her every move in their favor. Either she does not notice, or she simply does not care."

"And who is the reliable source feeding you such vital information?"

"Lady Olivia. I assure you, I did not leave her behind because I wanted to part with her. She detests Anna nearly as much as I do."

"Well, not to put a damper on your spirits, but we've received word only today that the empress has formally sent 62,000 troops to take Azov."

He slides the netter across the desk. I scan it, feeling my cheeks flush.

"Already at full-scale war with the Ottomans, and now this? What does she hope to gain?"

"I think she will not rest until all of Crimea is out from under the Turks and under our control once again."

After balling up the paper, I throw it into the fireplace. Landing among the cooling embers of the dying flames, it only smolders.

"A waste of men and resources. We cannot hold the fort for long, not with Austria already being beaten and Prussia making deals with the Turks behind our backs. A treaty must be made—soon—before the soldiers starve. Or, even worse, before they all contract the plague sweeping across the region."

"It's a show of force, meant more to bolster her image than anything. What does she care if we lose a few thousand soldiers to her vanity?"

"She is the empress. It is her *duty* to care."

"And yet, she does not. So, what will you do? Seek to counsel her on the matter?"

"She would not listen to my counsel in any case. No, we will send what we can in support of the troops—provisions, medicines. I'll have an accounting made up today, then send it to Azov. Hopefully, it will supply some relief."

"When do you plan to move against Anna?"

he asks pointedly, his voice lowered to a whisper. "Surely that is still your plan?"

I fold my hands below my chin. "I have nearly every piece I require in place. I am only waiting for the right moment. At this time, she is strong. Though the lords have already come to hate her, the people—the church in particular—are fond of her. I do not suspect she will hold their favor for long, especially in light of recent events. Once they turn, I'll make my move."

Shifting, I gaze out the window. I wait, muscles tense, to hear his reply.

"The regiment here is loyal to you, the true Romanov heir."

"They are, but I fear that is not enough. She has the loyalty of the church. Plus, the majority of the army follows her directions. I will need to sever both ties—as well as the support she enjoys from Prussia and Austria—if I am to make this bid."

"Gaining the church to your side will be a difficult task. How do you plan to turn them from her?"

Sitting back, I wave my hand, "I will do nothing. She will. Anna has always been her own worst enemy. For now, I will stay here and remain silent. We will know when it is the right time to move."

"And for the foreign allies?"

"I have already sent an envoy to Prussia, though I fear it is a lost cause. Anna is practically his puppet now, so nothing I can offer will be of more benefit.

As for Austria, they are in the midst of an upheaval of their own. I will wait to see the outcome before approaching them."

"Patience, then," he says with a grin, tilting his chin downward.

"In all things," I say. "But the canal?"

"Nearly complete. Ten new ships as well."

"Excellent. Please see that each worker receives a generous bonus for their efforts. And the army should receive new uniforms as well."

"Do we have the funds for that?"

"We do. I convinced the empress we needed to secure the fleet to make a grand show of her strength to the world. She agreed."

"Her strength... or yours?" He quirks a brow, and I have to laugh at his expression.

Quickly sobering, I continue, "At the moment, both. Which is why, this evening, I plan to open the palace to not just the nobles, but also the soldiers and commoners as well. A spring feast will bring some much-needed revelry to St. Petersburg."

"Full bellies and warm hearts will go a long way to earning you the favor of the people."

"And, to be honest, I simply cannot wait to see you in a gown," I add wickedly.

"Ah, yes, the dresses you've made available for the men are quite attractive, though I dare say I worry how you will look in a man's suit."

"Are you afraid it might not be appealing to the

eye, Sergei?"

"Just the opposite, in fact."

"It was Lady Lia's idea, but I admit, I enjoy the novelty of it. We shall see how comfortable the men are when they are the ones in corsets and hoop skirts."

Sergei chuckles, and the sound warms me to my toes.

"It will be a spectacle, I'm sure."

"That's the idea."

Chapter Two

As evening falls, Lady Lia helps me into my uniform. It's strikingly similar to an outfit my father used to favor. Made from velvet, it's a deep emerald color with lace lapels. It's formfitting enough there can be no mistaking the swell of my breasts or the curves of my hips, even after the sword and scabbard are fastened around me. My golden hair is curled, then tied at the nape of my neck with a ribbon, my usual tiara replaced by a general's hat. The jubilant sounds of the string quartet echo through the halls beyond as the first of my guests arrive.

"Lia, do you have my gift?"

Smirking, she retrieves a simple black box from my dresser, then hands it to me.

"It was delivered this morning."

Opening the box, I study the brass compass nestled into the red fabric. I had it engraved, but I do not need to flip it over to remember what it says.

For the one who has always been my true north.

"He will adore it," Lia whispers as she plays with her suspenders.

"I believe he will."

I pull Lia to my side. She appears quite masculine in her brown-and-tan garb with a leather huntsman belt. "Look at the pair of us."

"Your beauty cannot be hidden, even in trousers," she says, tugging at her jacket. "Yet, I look too much like a man."

Rocking back on my heels, I examine her. Since she confided her true nature, I haven't seen her as anything other than my favorite lady, friend, and confidant. But now, her broad shoulders and square jaw—features that would usually betray her—are on display.

"Lia, if you don't want to do this... If you are too uncomfortable with it—"

She shakes her head. "No, no. I wouldn't have suggested it if that were the case. I suppose it's just that—being here for so long, finally able to live as my true self—it's a reminder of how far I've come. And how incredibly grateful I am to have found a friend in you."

Taking her by the hands, I pull her into an embrace. "I am grateful for you as well. And I swear you will always have a home here where you can be completely yourself, without judgment."

"I appreciate that, Your Grace."

"Now, do you think we got it right?" I ask,

studying my reflection once more. "Do you think the resemblance is strong enough?"

"I think no one will be able to look upon you and not be reminded of your father."

"Then, that will have to do."

Together, we make our way to the grand staircase where Sergei waits. Upon seeing him, I cannot contain the giggle that escapes. His muscular shoulders are nearly bare, while his torso is wrapped in red satin with massive skirts jutting out from his waist. With his cheeks rouged and a smear of bright red lip color, he's still devastatingly handsome, chin square with his black beard neatly trimmed. Even as he bats his eyelashes coyly, the sight of him stirs me. I strut toward him the way a man might, and he takes my arm.

"It is as I feared, Lizzie. I am only grateful these skirts serve to hide my excitement well."

Laughing again, I lean in and whisper, "I do hope to see the evidence of that enthusiasm later."

When the herald announces us, we make our way down the stairs. Cheers erupt from the waiting crowd. As I scan their faces, I see the recognition flickering there. They know who I am.

I am the daughter of Tsar Peter.

The one rightful queen.

And I will spend the rest of my days reminding them of that fact.

As the evening winds on and the wine flows in seemingly endless fonts, even the few men who seemed abashed by the dress at first soon relax and begin to embrace the absurdity of the night. Dancing and eating, with no titles or rank to impede them, they lose themselves in the merriment.

Monsieur Sievers, a tall, slender young man who had overseen the construction of a few new fountains, twirls me into an enthusiastically drunken polonaise. Before long, he steps on the hem of his gown and entangles himself in it, pitching forward and managing to take us both to the ground. Helplessly, we laugh while others struggle to assist us. His skirt pops upward, taking down yet another lady in trousers, hopelessly trapping us ladies beneath it.

Finally, after a few more moments of tussling, we manage to right ourselves. In a flash, Sergei takes me by the waist, whisking me off for another dance before I can even catch my breath.

"I have not seen you laugh so in some time," he muses as we twirl. "It's good to see. I was afraid you'd forgotten how."

"As was I," I admit sheepishly, having a hard time remembering when I'd last felt so…carefree.

It had been with Peter. Of course it had. *Peter*…

"Oh, there's a frown I know too well."

Forcing a smile, I wonder if I will ever be good enough at pretending to be fine so that even Sergei will believe it.

"I know how difficult things have been for you since..." He hesitates. "Well, since recently. But I am here. If only you'd let me, I would do anything to make life better for you."

"You do make my life better," I say. "Whatever scraps of joy my heart still possess come only from being near you."

I only wish that were enough.

"Lizzy," he murmurs against my ear, one hand trailing down my back. My flesh tingles beneath his touch.

How easy it is to lose myself in him, I realize. How thoroughly he's able to part the storms raging inside my mind.

"I have something for you. I left it in my room. Will you meet me there later tonight?"

Although I cannot see it, I feel his grin next to my ear.

"As if I could deny you anything."

Extricating myself from his hold as gently as possible, I straighten. "Then, I shall see you later. For now, I should continue to greet my guests."

"You should. Or..."

Seizing me once more, he drags me to a darkened corner. He presses himself against me before lowering his mouth to mine.

"Someone will see," I protest weakly.

"Let them see."

He kisses me gently at first, nipping at my bottom lip with his teeth before deepening the embrace, his tongue dancing across my own. He tastes like bitter wine and candied almonds. For the life of me, I can't muster up the will to push him away. The stubble of his beard tickles my chin. When he finally draws back, I have to gasp for air.

Wiping his thumb across my lips, he shows me the lip paint smeared on its pad before gently pressing it into my mouth for me to suckle.

When I do, teasing it with my tongue, he groans, his eyes fluttering closed.

Finally, I playfully bite down, and his green eyes open, hooded and desperate.

"You are the sweetest torment," he murmurs, pulling his hand away and licking his thumb.

"Then I will torment you no longer. For now," I tease, pushing him back a step and making my escape.

The feast goes on until half the court has either retired or are asleep where they fell, sprawled across settees and chairs, some even leaned over tables still full of food. Lia helps me to my room, but I dismiss her quickly, opting to change myself. If she wonders why, she does not ask. Bidding me goodnight, she simply slips to her chamber next door. Around my room, candles have been lit, creating a dim flickering glow.

My outer room door opens and closes with a soft click, then the snick of a lock echoes before my inner door creaks open and Sergei enters. He's abandoned his gown for a simple pair of tan trousers and a soft white tunic, which hangs open around his neck to expose a hint of dark chest hair. I'm brushing my hair at my vanity when his reflection appears in the mirror. Plucking the brush from my fingers, he begins stroking it down my golden tresses.

"It's late," I say.

"It's early," he corrects with a grin.

"I was beginning to think you'd forgotten about me."

"No, you weren't."

"Or that perhaps you'd found some other lady to spend the evening with."

"Well, Lord Blackbourne *did* look quite fetching in that peach gown…"

Closing my eyes, I let my head lull to the side as he strokes the bristles through my hair. Finally, he leans forward and kisses the side of my neck. The feel of his warm lips on my flesh sends shivers through me.

"But, as always, there is only one lady I wish to

spend my evening with."

Lifting me from my seat, he carries me to my bed, depositing me gently among the soft blankets.

With deliberately slow fingers, he draws my nightgown up my legs, over my torso, and finally over my head, leaving me bare and crawling with goose flesh.

"Are you cold?"

I laugh. "I am now."

"Shall I warm you?"

"It seems only fair," I agree, grabbing the front of his tunic and yanking him on top of me.

Chapter Three

Afterward, we lay together for some time as he trails his fingertips across my bare back, cradling me against him.

"I didn't even get to give you your gift," I murmur, sighing with drowsy contentment.

"Oh, I assure you that you did," he teases, kissing the tip of my nose.

Pulling away for only a moment, I retrieve the box before curling back into his warmth.

"For your name day," I murmur, handing it to him.

"You didn't have to get me a gift."

"Of course I did. I think thirty years of this world having you in it is something to celebrate. Not that you look a day past twenty. How is it that you stay so young while I get so old?"

"Does it bother you? Then today, I shall live my last. I shall never grow a moment beyond this, so I may preserve this moment forever." Lowering his lips to mine, he kisses me desperately, the taste of him on my tongue the sweetest torment.

Only when I push away does he grin and open the box. He pulls out the compass, running his thumb over the engraving.

"Though, for the record, you will never be old in my eyes. I will always see you as I did the first time we met."

"Even when I'm wrinkled and grey?" I ask.

"Especially then..." He laughs, and I slap him playfully.

"But, truly, I love it," he says sheepishly.

"I'm glad. I know it isn't jewels or—"

He cuts me off with another kiss.

"It's perfect."

He props up on one elbow, brushes the hair off the side of my face, and gazes down at me.

"Marry me, Lizzy."

Just as quickly as my heart leaps for joy, it sinks like a stone, crashing in my chest.

"Sergei..."

"I know, Lizzy. I know all the reasons you think you can't or shouldn't. But don't you see? None of it matters. Together, we can write our own destiny."

"We are together."

"Be my wife. Make an honest man out of me," he jokes, kissing my ear. "Please, Lizzy. I love you. I've loved you since the first time I laid eyes on you when you were meant to wed Charles. Even then, I wanted you more than I've ever wanted anyone or anything."

"Anna would never allow it."

"Then marry me in secret. No one but us ever needs to know."

When I don't answer, he sighs. "Twice, Lizzy, I have stood by and watched as you gave your heart to other men. Twice, I've seen it broken in the cruelest ways. But now, we are here. Together. We have a chance to live a wonderful life with each other. I will spend every day for the rest of mine loving you and making you happy—if you will only let me."

"I know you would," I whisper, unable to deny the truth of his words.

"But?"

"But you know I cannot."

"Because you cannot give me a child? Do you think such a thing makes me want you any less?"

Sitting up, I pull the blankets up, curling them to my chest.

"It is not only that. My country—my *people*—are suffering. I must claim the throne. There's simply no way I can do that as your wife—or as *anyone's* wife. Even if I choose to give up my claim, I would forever be a contender, a threat to be eliminated. My love carries a death sentence, Sergei, one even a *king* could not survive."

"I would take that chance."

"But I would not. I have already lost my family, my fiancé, even Peter. Sergei, I could not bear another heartbreak. I could not love you only to lose you. Please, ask anything else of me except that."

"Lizzy," he protests, rising to sit beside me. He presses a tender kiss to my shoulder.

"No," I say firmly. "I mean it, Sergei. Someday, I will lose you. I feel it in my bones. Whether to accident, catastrophe, or to the arms of another, I know it as surely as I know the sun will rise tomorrow."

"If you don't want to lose me, then do not push me away."

"I must. This is as close as I can hold you, but no closer. I know this hurts you—it hurts me as well—but it's best to suffer a little hurt now than to be destroyed by it later."

Throwing the covers back, Sergei rolls from the bed, dressing in a huff. "You have already broken me, Elizabeth. You have broken me in ways I never imagined possible. Yet, I love you still. When my heart beats, the sound it makes is your name. That will not change. No matter how you protest or how you rage, my heart is yours. You cut your teeth on it, yet it remains yours still."

"How you must hate me," I whisper, blinking back the tears threatening to escape my eyes.

"It would be easier if I did, but it's not like I ever could."

"I'm sorry."

Such a weak phrase, but it's so absolutely true.

If I could be someone else for him, anyone else, I would. But I am a queen, if not by title, then by blood and birth. No amount of wishing can change that.

"I am stronger than you give me credit for. No accident or catastrophe, much less another woman, could ever take me from you. I only wish you had faith in me."

"It is not a matter of faith," I counter. "But I will not condemn myself with false hope ever again. And I will not condemn you to it, either."

He approaches me, his expression dark as he stares into my eyes. Finally, resigned, he presses a kiss to my forehead and exits my room without another word, leaving me alone with my cold bed and an empty heart.

Chapter Four

The nightmares come again, robbing me of sleep and sanity. Each is worse than the last—images of Count Osterman's severed head morphing into that of others. When I scream, no words escape my throat. I can't breathe. Can't move. I'm frozen in a moment of fear and agony. Someone calls my name. *Sergei.* I turn to him, but I find myself staring at the gallows instead. After pushing through the crowd, I discover him on his knees with his arms chained, his expression anguished as he watches—*me*. I'm on the gallows. Being forced to kneel, I am roughly shoved, head down, on the block. I'm crying out his name as the ax falls…

And then I wake, startled and alone.

Every muscle in my body aches, my throat is raw, and my hair is matted to my face with sweat and tears.

Every night, the dreams plague me. Even Lia's tonic can't keep them at bay for long.

This morning, I find a letter waiting on my bed

after I manage to calm my racing heart. I open it, dreading what it might say. When had it been delivered? Had a stranger been in my room even as I dreamed about losing my head?

"Lia," I call, and she rushes in.

"Yes, Your Grace?"

"Where did this come from?" I ask, waving the missive in the air.

She glances around, then lowers her voice before answering. "It came early this morning by personal messenger. It's from Lady Olivia, I believe."

I rip the seal, unfolding the letter, then skim it. Surely, she'd send me a warning if Anna had made some formal move against me.

Princess Elizabeth,

It has been a long while since we last spoke. I wanted you to know I'm being dispatched to Holstein in the coming days. Our empress prefers the company of her German ladies, and she informed me I am no longer needed here. To be honest, this comes as a relief. I never imagined I would tire of the frivolous games of court, but I've had more than my fill recently. Even the empress seems bored of late. She doesn't even dance anymore. Mostly, she just sits upon her throne, stone-faced, seeming to wait to pass judgment on anyone for even the slightest infraction.

Lately, you have become a topic of much discussion

here at court. Not from Empress Anna herself, of course, but from the other nobles. Often, they'll speak of how things used to be under your father's rule while remarking on how much light you used to bring to court. They speak of missing the golden Romanovs. These whispers displease the empress to no end. I have no doubt she will soon tire of them—one way or another. A storm hovers over Moscow, and I fear it might be moving in your direction. Though, knowing you, you'll simply stand out in the pouring rain until you charm the sun into shining once again.

One last thing...I have started a rumor around court that Sergei is a eunuch. Rumors you had taken him as your lover were floating around, so I simply laughed and remarked it could not be true, due to his unfortunate condition. I do not know whether the empress believes the rumor, but the story has gripped the court. Please send him my apologies. I only did it to keep you both safe. Although I must admit, it has given me hours of amusement.

All my love,
Olivia

After folding the letter, I hold it over a candle until it catches the flame, then toss it into the fire. I can't help but grin as I picture what Sergei's expression will be when I inform him about the details of his now-tarnished reputation.

Even so, her words bother me. A storm is coming—and even robbing Sergei of his manhood cannot keep it at bay.

I take my time dressing, opting to spend some time outdoors. Lia and I take a walk around the gardens, basking in the warmth of the sun.

"So, what news did Olivia impart?" Lia asks as we stroll past the bubbling fountains.

I grin. "Apparently, she has begun a rumor Sergei is a eunuch."

Lia giggles, nearly doubling over. "I believe he will be most disturbed to hear that."

"I'm sure he will. Amusing as it is, she fears for us. With each passing day, Anna's jealousy grows more venomous. Olivia fears for us. She writes that a storm is coming."

"Ominous. However, it's not unexpected, is it?"

"No, it's not." I frown. "I am so tired, Lia. I am weary of the constant struggle to keep the people I love safe. It's been a burden I've carried my entire life, it seems."

"I think," she begins, obviously choosing her words carefully, "that all we can do is accept our struggles for what they are. But we still must remember to seek joy in the small moments between. If you are always fighting for your life, you need must not forget to live it as well."

Releasing my arm, she wanders to one of the fountains. Its surface is covered with thick green pads and lotus. She plucks a bright pink bloom, then brings it back and tucks it behind my ear.

"The ancient people believe the lotus flower is a symbol of strength. No matter how long and dark the winter may be, they always return in the spring, as vibrant and thick as before," she says, taking my arm once more. "Women are like that. They blossom and fade in their season, but once their roots take hold, they always find their way back to the sun. Fragile, like a flower, but strong and resilient."

"I must admit, I do not think Anna is fragile as a flower."

"Anna? No," she teases. "She is not fragile like a flower. Mayhap, I think she's fragile like gunpowder."

Laughing, we continue our stroll before heading inside.

Sergei is deep in conversation with a palace guard when we return. As I approach, his face sets in a scowl.

"What is it?" I ask urgently.

He shakes his head. "Emperor Charles of Austria has died. Despite their alliance, the French are moving against the Hapsburgs."

I sigh. "Of course they are."

"We will have little to no involvement at this point, but I'm increasing palace security just to be safe."

"Always my diligent protector."

He bows.

"Come, take a ride with me. It's lovely today, and I would like to discuss the news I received from Moscow."

He raises one eyebrow.

"Have the horses prepared. I'm going to change," I say.

When he bows again, I think he understands my reluctance to speak openly. Besides wanting the privacy, I do want to settle the air between us. I hate the way our last encounter left my emotions off-kilter. I'm hoping to reconcile, at least a bit, before the storm Olivia warned me about arrives.

We ride west, crossing the river, then head deep into the forest beyond. I'm not sure how much ground we cover, only that the wind in my hair and the powerful flanks of my horse carry me away from my troubling thoughts. We finally stop in an open grove of trees where a meadow of tall grasses and wild crocuses stretches out before us. It's a place I remember well. Peter and I used to come here from time to time. It took us far from the pressures and demands of court, with not another soul around for miles. Riding up to my side, Sergei affectionately pats his winded mare.

"You were right. It's the perfect day for a ride."

I grin, stretching my hands skyward. "It is, isn't

it? I love it here. It feels so far removed from my troubles."

"As much as I hate to ask, what news did you want to share with me?"

I feel the corners of my mouth tilt up before I can stop them. "According to the rumors flying in Anna's court, you have been quite robbed of your manhood."

His face twists, brows furrowing.

"Olivia," I explain. "She feared Anna was growing suspicious of our relationship, so she started a rumor…"

"That I've been emasculated?" He considers it for a moment. "I can't decide whether to be appreciative or offended."

"A bit of both would be completely understandable."

He waves the rumor away, his expression sobering.

"Lizzy, I would like to talk about the other night," he begins, his tone serious.

"As would I. I hate feeling there is such distance between us."

"I should not have asked you to marry me. I already knew what your answer and your reasonings would be. Maybe I do not completely agree with them, but I do understand," he offers.

"And I should not have been so harsh with you. It's just that every time I've opened myself up to love, it has devastated me, and it has cost more than one good man their life. And so I hold myself back, but not to hurt you. Quite the opposite, in fact."

"You still believe Anna will come for you?"

"She must," I reply with a shrug. "Eventually, either she, or someone on her behalf, will come for me. It is nothing less than a war between us. Only one of us will survive the fallout—of that, I am absolutely certain."

"Then we must make sure it's you."

Sidling up beside me, he leans over. Eagerly, I meet him for a long, deep kiss.

When I finally draw back, breathless, my horse begins to fidget restlessly beneath me.

I hear the *whoosh* of an arrow cutting through the air before I see it. It pierces through Sergei's leg. He cries out, shifting to shield me with his body. Horrified, I frantically scan the area.

"Go, Elizabeth. *Now*," Sergei orders.

Another arrow whooshes by, its target Sergei's chest. When it hits its mark, he pitches forward on his horse, the reins falling from his hands.

"Sergei!"

"*Go*," he orders again.

Fury bubbling through me, I search the trees for our assailant. My gaze lands upon a lone archer in a tattered leather hunting jacket, a scraggly, full beard hiding his face. When he realizes I've spotted him, he jumps up from his hiding spot behind a fallen tree and runs.

Spurring my horse, I give chase, drawing my knife from the belt of my riding trousers. With each beat of my heart, my rage courses stronger within me. I know I should flee, but my only thought at the moment is revenge. My horse leaps the fallen log with ease as I push it through the dense thicket. The archer is quick, but no match for me on horseback. Just as he turns to loose an arrow at me, I leap from the saddle, tackling him to the ground. Tumbling down the side of a grassy slope, we land in a tangled heap. I throw myself on top of him, pinning him to the ground before he manages to grab for his bow. When I press my blade to the fragile skin of his throat, he stills.

"Who sent you?" I demand.

The archer shakes his head, saying nothing. He doesn't have to. Fear rolls off him like the stench of a pig. He bucks, thinking to throw me, but I hold fast, digging my blade deeper into his neck until the first crimson drop appears.

"You tell your empress she will take nothing else from me. Not on this day, nor on any other."

Wordlessly stammering, he nods, but my rage has not yet cooled.

"Never mind," I decide, briefly lifting the blade to slice into his neck from ear to ear, in one clean motion. "I'll tell her myself."

When I stand, he flops to his side, fingers

scrabbling at his neck as he tries to crawl away. Dispassionately, I watch until the last of his energy leaves him. He goes still, the last of his lifeblood flowing across the grass and into the stream below.

How dare she do this. How dare she come for me. For Sergei.

Sergei.

I race to my horse. Quickly, I mount, then force the animal into a full-out gallop. Sergei comes into view. Panting, he leans forward, his breathing shallow.

"Sergei," I call. He lifts his head, his features tightened into a mask of pain. "Can you ride?"

He groans, but nods. I grab his reins, leading his horse to the palace as quickly as I dare.

Not thinking about the blood drying on my hands or even the man I left behind, I only pray Sergei will be all right.

A storm is coming.

That's what Oliva's warning predicted.

But, eventually, all storms run out of rain. And when this one does, I plan to burn Anna and any who would defend her to the ground.

Chapter Five

The guards help me get Sergei inside. I clean Sergei's wounds the best I can, afraid to remove the arrow embedded in his leg. When I inspect his chest, however, I breathe a sigh of relief. The arrow had hit the compass I'd given him and sheared off, making the wound shallow enough for me to deal with on my own. Luckily, he'd been carrying it in his breast pocket. Otherwise…

I hold the brass compass in my hand, closing my fingers around it with a prayer of thanks.

Soon, the doctor arrives. Sergei fades in and out, his face pale and matted with sweat, his chest heaving with the effort to simply breathe past the pain. Lia arrives with a knife, a basin of fresh water, and a few rags. We set about removing his clothes. Though the shot to his chest had mostly missed, his rib beneath is already forming a wide, dark bruise.

After sticking a bit of wood between Sergei's teeth for him to clamp down on against the pain, the doctor carefully removes the last arrow from his leg. It draws a muffled scream from Sergei. I sit beside him, combing his hair with my fingers in an attempt to soothe him. His back arches, and he finally collapses with a grunt.

"He's lost a great deal of blood," the doctor says as he washes the wound.

"Will he survive?" I ask, my voice trembling.

It's Lia who answers. "Of course he will."

Although she's clearly trying to be encouraging, I can't help but frown at her.

"I will do my best," the doctor says.

"Do better than that," I demand.

"Come, Your Grace. Let's leave him to his work," Lia offers.

Leaning over Sergei, whose eyes have fluttered closed again, I whisper, "I'll be right outside, pacing a trough in the floors. Do not leave me, Sergei. I beg you. You are my entire heart, my love."

After kissing his forehead, I rise and leave the room, pacing just beyond the door as I'd promised.

"I can't lose him, Lia," I say weakly.

"You won't."

"It's my fault," I continue. "Olivia tried to warn me that Anna was reaching her vile hand in our direction."

"You could not have known this would happen."

"But I knew *something* would. It always does. It is my curse. Everything and everyone I love is taken from me."

Coming to my side, she clasps my hands between her own. "I know it feels that way now, but you're not cursed. Nor are you to blame."

I can't think clearly. I'm far too angry for that. All the rage, fear, and worry bubble up inside me in a ceaseless tide, drowning everything else.

"You must send the guard to find the person who did this," she says.

Shaking my head, I pull my hands from hers. "I already have. I chased him down like the vile animal he was, then cut his throat with my own hands."

If she's shocked by my admission, she does not show it. Her face remains neutral. "Did he admit to his actions being on the empress' orders?"

"He said nothing."

"Then you have done all you can. Come now, let's go clean you up. You would not wish to greet Sergei looking like this."

"I cannot leave him," I protest. "If he…"

I can't finish the thought. Instead, I crumple into her arms. We both fall to our knees, where she holds me. As I sob, she prays.

Minutes turn to hours as the sun begins to set. My knees ache, but the tears have already dried on my cheeks when the doctor finally leaves the room. Numbly, I can only stare up at him as I wait for the news.

"I have cleaned and stitched the wound. There is nothing more I can do now but wait to see how he progresses. But I think he will recover."

Without another thought, I leap to my feet and throw my arms around the old doctor. Awkwardly, he pats me on the back.

"Yes, well. He should rest now. See to it the bandages are changed often. If he becomes feverish, fetch me at once."

"I will, thank you," I promise, releasing him.

"I'll have the kitchen send up some bone broth and wine. He will need to keep his strength up," the doctor adds. Respectfully, he bows before taking his leave.

"Lia, please have the maids run me a bath, then bring extra bandages to his room to have them ready. I'll bathe and change before I sit with him."

"Of course, Your Grace."

Cracking the door open, I find Sergei sleeping once again, his leg bandaged tightly and elevated on a stack of pillows. Heart overflowing, I let myself stand there, watching him in silence, until the maids arrive with his tray.

Taking it in myself, I set it next to his bed, then caress his pale cheek.

Whether the arrow was meant for him or me, I do not know. But I vow I will never allow anything to wound him—not ever again.

Chapter Six

The servants bring a chaise from my chamber so I may nap by his side when I tire, but I spend most of my time reading to Sergei in between restless fits. His leg is swollen and red, but there's been no fever, nor any smell of decay. The doctor checks on him every other day, more for my sake than his, I think. Sergei is twice bled with leeches before I put a stop to the treatment, for each session seems to leave him paler and weaker than the last.

My ladies take to dressing and bathing me in his room since I refuse to leave him for anything other than using the privy chamber. I keep watch over him, hoping he'll open his eyes and try to peek at me as I undress, but he does not. It's days before his emerald eyes open again, and I can finally draw a full breath into my lungs.

"Ovid?" he asks weakly. "I'm on my deathbed… and you read me Ovid?"

Closing the book and setting it aside, I hurry to his side. "I'd hoped some of his more scandalous poems would rouse you."

The corners of his mouth turn up ever so slightly. "Cruel thing to do, teasing a eunuch."

"I will do much worse if you ever think to leave me again," I threaten.

"Never. Come, lay beside me. I would like to feel the warmth of you, if only so I can be sure I'm not dreaming."

As he requests, I stretch out along the length of him, curling as close as I dare without jostling his leg. Nuzzling into his chest, I take a deep breath, savoring his familiar scent. He kisses my forehead gently.

"Ah, real. I'm glad."

"Were your dreams so disappointing?"

"I only dreamt of you."

His words are so weak and sad that the very sound makes my heart ache.

"What did you dream?" I whisper.

He licks his lips. "I dreamt we were on a ship at sea, just the two of us. The wind was blowing through your hair, and I could taste salt on your lips. I dreamt that you chose me, loved me, and we traveled far away from this place..." He trails off, probably expecting me to protest or rebuke him. But I do neither. I haven't the heart for it now.

"It sounds like a beautiful dream. I'm sorry you had to leave it."

"No dream is better than the reality of holding

you again. Ah, but you should not have risked yourself to come back for me. I told you to flee."

"When have you ever known me to do as I was told?" I ask, cradling his face in my hand.

Shifting, he places a kiss in my palm. "I'm glad you didn't. The shock of it alone may have killed me."

"You are not allowed to die. Didn't you know? I've forbidden it. And you cannot disobey me."

"You're not the empress yet."

"Does it matter?"

"No," he admits. "Not to me."

"Then obey me now, Sergei, and rest."

"Will you stay?" he asks, his voice growing drowsy.

"I would not leave you for anything. Now sleep, my love, and dream of better things."

The days roll on. With each new dawn, Sergei grows stronger. It isn't long until he's restless and sore from his long confinement. I help him stand, but only to walk around the room a few times a day while he grumbles.

"This is torture," he mutters grumpily as I settle him back in bed.

"Are you so tired of my company already?" I

tease.

"Never that. Only of this bed and this room and these walls."

"You're wound is healing well. No doubt you'll be back on a horse soon enough. For now, I'm quite enjoying having you all to myself."

"You're enjoying this too much."

I shrug. "Perhaps. It is nice knowing *you* need *me* for once."

"Ah, I always need you."

"No, you always *want* me," I correct him. "Need is a different beast entirely."

"I could ask for no better nurse, truly. But tell me of other affairs. How are things in Moscow?"

"The empress is in Poland, vying against the treaty. Things seem to have calmed in her absence, though I believe she'll be returning soon. In this matter, she cannot force her will, which will make her temper all the worse when she does."

"And she can't be pleased her attempt on your life failed so miserably," he adds.

"No, I'm certain she isn't. She will have to come at me directly now. However, it would be a terrible risk for her, politically speaking. To attack me without provocation would only further anger the few remaining nobles, and I doubt the church would stand for it."

"You allot her too much credit. She gives no such forethought to her actions. I fear she believes herself so far above them that she pays them no mind at all."

"And yet, you cannot hope to rule the country for long without their support."

That is one of the many lessons my father taught me. A king with powerful allies at his back is a force to be reckoned with. But a king on his own is weak and vulnerable.

Sergei takes my hand. Pulling me down next to him, he kisses my forehead. "You are right, as always."

"I am afraid, Sergei," I admit. "More afraid than I was even during her massacre of a coronation. I'm afraid she'll stop at nothing to take you from me."

"She has tried, and she failed. If she tries again, she will still fail. Because you and I are bonded. And it's something no ax can sever, nor any arrow can pierce."

He kisses me again. This time, his lips meet mine, tender and sweet. Soon, the heat between us rises, his kisses growing desperate and frenzied.

When I pull away, he growls.

"No," I say. "You are not yet well enough for that."

"I think you'll find I'm always well enough for that."

Sighing, I kiss the tip of his nose. "Soon," I promise. "Rest now."

"I'm so rested I may not need sleep for a hundred years."

"Then we have a hundred long nights to look

forward to, once you're on your feet."

"I'll hold you to that," he replies with a sly grin.

Just then, a page arrives, bowing from his position in the threshold.

"Your Grace," he says as I rise. "There's a messenger here for you. From France."

I frown before I can think better of it. "Of course, please have him wait in my study. I'll be along momentarily."

"Take a guard," Sergei orders, struggling to sit up.

"I will if you promise to rest."

After he agrees, I reluctantly take my leave from his chambers.

The messenger waits in the study, his posture stern, his hands folded across his lap.

"What is it?" I ask.

"I have a message for you from Duke Stanisław."

"Where is it?" I ask, holding my hand out for a letter.

He shakes his head. "It may only be given by voice. He personally relayed the message to me. I'm forbidden from speaking it in front of anyone, save you."

"How odd," I remark, taking a seat. Stanisław is the former king of Poland, where our empress now finds herself. When he'd been deposed, he'd fled to France. "What does he wish to tell me?"

"Duke Stanisław asks me to relate his affections.

Furthermore, he wishes to serve notice there is no ill will between himself and the Noble House of Romanov, should it require his assistance."

"Then he should be making this statement to the empress."

"He says he, too, understands the tragedy of losing one's rightful crown to a usurper. And he would ease your troubles in any way he can, should the need arise."

"Stanisław holds the city of Lorraine, does he not?" I ask.

The messenger nods. "And Bar as well."

"Under the authority of the French crown?"

"Yes, Your Grace."

I tap my fingers on the desk. Whether the offer is genuine or a trap, there is no way to know. It's far more likely, however, that he's looking for revenge on the Russian forces who defeated his claim. A divided Russia is an easy target for France and her allies.

"I shall pen my response. Thank you."

I dismiss him with a wave, then set about crafting my letter.

Duke Stanisław,

I am glad to hear you have settled comfortably in your new Duchy, and I appreciate the offer of comfort and aid you've so kindly sent. However, I must advise you not to contact me again. This matter, as with all matters of national security and trust, can only be delivered to our great Empress Anna. We are well provided for here, and we have no desires for, nor intentions to make, upon her throne. I live only to serve my nation and its sovereign leader.

I do not mean for my rebuke to sound harsh, but these are difficult times. Even a whisper of rebellion must be quashed firmly and quickly lest it grows to stain us all. I cannot imagine your offer could be interpreted any other way than as an act of aggression, no matter how tender the intent. I would caution you against seeking to stir division among us, as any such action must be met with the harshest punishments.

Her Majesty's humble servant,
Princess Elizabeth Romanova

Signed and sealed, I deliver my note to the messenger, who bows before taking his leave.

"What was all that?" Lady Lia asks, approaching from the stairs.

"Truthfully, I'm not certain."

I cannot help but think if France truly wished to offer its support to me, it would have been done privately, through Lia herself. Most likely, it wasn't Stanislaw's man at all, but the empress trying to ensnare me in a treasonous plot. A pitiful ruse, at best. And if the offer were, indeed, genuine, I would not seek support from Duke Stanisław in any case, as he only holds two small cities and has no army or wealth to speak of. No, when I am ready, I will go directly to King Louis for support.

Besides, I would not give Anna the satisfaction of fooling me so easily, not when I'm confident she's plotting against me.

"If you'll excuse me, Lia, I should return to Sergei."

"Yes, before he ties the linens together, then flees from his window," she offers with a smile. "He is recovering well enough, Your Grace. You cannot keep him locked in his lavish prison forever."

"It is not a prison," I protest.

"It is to him. I understand your fear and desire to keep him safe, but you cannot keep him chained like a dog. It will only end up making him crazy."

How well she sees through me. She's right, of course. But even the thought of letting Sergei out of my sight makes me uneasy.

"He is not a wounded bird, after all. Sergei is a strong man—a soldier. You cannot ask him to be any less."

"I know you are right, but I do not know if I can bear it."

"You must," Lia says. "Bury whatever fears you have, and only show him a brave face. It is the only way."

I take her offered arm, and she walks me to his

room. “All right, but I’m going to hate every second of it.”

“I’d expect no less. Perhaps you can soothe yourself—and Sergei, as well—by making his first outing a private one…”

“Devious. What are you thinking?”

“Take him to the Summer Palace. It has been opened for the season. The setting is small, intimate even. A few days away would do you both some good. You need to inspect the palace, anyway, so make an excursion of it. But send an advance guard to secure the area first.”

The Summer Palace is the humble home my father had built for my mother. Before they were married, he would take her there. He used it as an escape from the pressures of life at court. After they were wed, they returned each year on the anniversary of their wedding. I’d only been a few times in my youth, but I remember being so impressed with how wonderfully peaceful the place felt.

“Yes, that’s an excellent idea. I’ll tell Sergei at once.”

Chapter Seven

The Summer Place feels like a beacon of brighter days to come, the way it glows a bright canary yellow under the morning sun as Sergei and I arrive. After he helps me from the carriage, he walks—limping slightly but unaided—inside and into the foyer. The décor is far from the opulence of the Winter Palace. Instead, it boasts only simple oak walls with carved reliefs of Minerva, Dutch tile, and simple stucco fireplaces. Surrounded by the Neva on three sides, there's a hint of salt in the breeze, the soft pulse of the river tide echoing through the halls. This is not the palace of a king—it's the home of a simple family. On the main level, I find my father's workshop. It's clean, but otherwise untouched, having not been used since the last time he'd stepped foot in it. I wander through it now, trailing my fingers over his tools, admiring the unfinished wooden carvings strewn about the table.

This place seems frozen in time, and I can almost hear his laughter echoing off the very walls.

"I must admit, this is not what I would have expected from a man like your father," Sergei muses as he joins me in the workshop.

I shake my head. "This was the heart of him. As much as he loved his gold and grandeur, his soul always longed for a simpler life. When he and my mother first wed, they lived here for some time. He made his carvings while she tended the gardens with her own hands. One might have thought them any normal couple instead of Russia's emperor and empress."

"It sounds lovely."

"It was a dream. Great men often dream of simple lives, I think, because it's the one thing they can never have. Eventually, even this had to be given up to the duty of the crown. That's all this place ended up being—a dream of something he could never truly possess. I have to wonder if having it for a while was worth the pain of losing it in the end."

I turn to Sergei, continuing. "But that's why we're here—to find out. I cannot offer you the life you want, Sergei, but I can give you a piece of it. A tiny dream to hold on to. Because once I take the crown, this will all fade away, as fate says it must."

Wrapping his arms around me, he presses our bodies tightly together. "Then I will take the dream while we may, even knowing I must let it go when the time comes."

With that promise spoken between us, he kisses

me.

Letting all the worries and weights drop from my shoulders, I fervently return his kisses, silently vowing to enjoy this time we have.

No matter what the future may hold.

It is most odd not having servants, though not wholly unpleasant. Outside, the guards man their posts, but within these walls, Sergei and I are the only occupants. He helps me dress, and I cook for him as best I can. I'm sure the meals I manage are mostly awful, but he never complains. Each morning, I collect eggs from the hens in the chicken coop while Sergei chops wood for the fireplaces. In the evenings, he reads to me by candlelight before taking me to his bed. Truthfully, he's as content as I've ever seen him, so I try to conceal my growing restlessness for his benefit. But being this far from the Winter Palace unnerves me. I feel as if I am missing vital information during our seclusion. What new rumors are being whispered at court? What duties am I letting fall by the wayside, unfinished, until my return? However, there has been one benefit from playing house like a simple commoner rather than the daughter of an emperor—I'm resting. Each night, my sleep is peaceful and dreamless. I know it's the constant rise and fall of Sergei's chest at my back, his arm holding me against the darkness, that allows my untroubled slumbers.

On our last morning, I wake to find he's already left our bed. I stretch in the warmth streaming through my window, wondering where he's disappeared to.

When he enters our chamber, he balances a tray of bread and coffee in one hand while gripping a basket in the other.

"What are you up to?" I ask, sitting upright as he leans in for a kiss.

"Well, since we must return to the Winter Palace today, I thought we should take a few things with us so we may remember our days spent here."

"As if I could ever forget a single moment."

Grinning, he sets the tray on the bed, then curls in behind me as he settles the basket in my lap.

"Open it."

When I pull back the lid, flowers from my mother's garden overflow from their confinement. Taking a handful, he sprinkles them through his fingers. "I thought we could dry them, then string them up in your room. So you can always have a bit of this place with you as you fall asleep. Let the memories of it chase the nightmares away."

As he presses a kiss to my bare shoulder, I twist in his arms, cradling his face in my palms.

I love you.

I nearly say the words aloud, but they catch in

my throat. As much as they are clawing to be free of me, I cannot give them a voice. It would be the worst fate I could set upon him. It's this place—it makes everything else feel so insignificant. But the real world awaits us outside, and it will not be so gentle there. To say it now would only mean having to deny it later, and I could never be so cruel. Not to Sergei—my guard, my friend, my *love*.

From his smile, I realize he's read the truth of it on my face. Feels, too, my fear.

"It's all right," he says, his voice soothing. "My love is strong enough for us both."

When he kisses me again, I cannot help but feel the strings of fate being plucked. Deep in my heart, the knowledge our time together is drawing to an end surges through me. The hurt that wells behind it is so visceral that I may as well have already lost him.

Chapter Eight

Once we return to real life, the next several weeks drone on in endless monotony. Sergei has not come to me again, even though his gaze lingers on me whenever we are together. Not able to take his cold shoulder any longer, I corner him in my office as he gathers the day's work.

"Sergei," I begin, the lines I've so carefully practiced abandoning me entirely as he focuses his attention on me. "Are you all right?"

He smirks. "Of course, Your Grace. Why wouldn't I be?"

"You have barely spoken to me in weeks."

He shrugs. "I have been…preoccupied."

"With what?"

His grin falters. "Admittedly, with anything I can think of to keep my mind off you. I'm trying to give you some space in hopes you'll miss me."

"I do desperately miss you. Every moment."

"I beg you not to say such things, Lizzy."

"Then tell me, Sergei, what would you have me

say? That I adore you? That I would run off with you in a second if I weren't carrying the burden of my nation on my shoulders? Because those are all true."

"I love you, Lizzy. Still. Forever." His voice is sad, resigned. He promised to return with me when I was ready, but I cannot help but think he's longing for the days we spent in the Summer Palace. Longing, too, for the dream I offered him only as a temporary respite to be permanent. But I'd been truthful with him from the start. I'd told him the fantasy could not last. Yet, it now seems as if he's punishing me because of it. Irritation rises inside me like a swelling tide.

"And did you imagine loving me would be easy? Were you under the delusion that loving a queen would be simple and uncomplicated? I did not think you were so foolish."

"Nothing about you is ever easy." He sighs. "It never has been."

His words are a rebuke, but they only fan the fire inside me.

"Then love me as I am, Sergei, or do not love me at all. I will offer you everything I'm able to, but do not ask for more. If you cannot accept me as I am, then leave me now to save me the pain of being close to you but not able to have you. But do not stay if you only wish to continue punishing me. I cannot do what must be done with my head and heart so wounded."

My tone is sharp, and my words come out flat. Even as the very idea of him leaving me tears up my insides, as I silently pray he won't go, I mean every word.

Before he can speak, the footman rushes in. Hurriedly, he bows, then straightens.

"Pardon me, Your Grace. A package from the empress has just arrived for you. I'm afraid it's quite urgent. The messenger said it is to be opened by you alone, on royal order."

"I'll be there in a moment," I say with a flick of my hand, not ready to abandon my current conversation just yet.

"Yes, uh…of course. I only thought you should know, because, *um*, it appears to be…"

"What?" I demand again.

"Bleeding."

Chapter Nine

With Sergei close behind me, I rush toward the kitchens where the basket has been carefully placed in a deep basin. The odor hits me first—rotted meat and curdled milk. It's so awful that flies buzz around it, and I have to put my hand over my mouth to keep from retching. As I examine the basket, I understand the footman's alarm. The blood-soaked wood is smeared with darker dry smudges. It is a truly macabre sight. A sealed letter, bearing the royal seal, has been tied to the basket in red twine.

Plucking the note free, I search for the cleanest spot to break the seal. Stomach in knots, because there is no way this news can be anything but terrible, I unfold it and read.

Cousin,

Excuse the informality of this letter, but I wanted to be sure the meaning was clear. Yesterday, after much interrogation, Minister Artemii Volynskii admitted to heading a plot against the crown. He and several named co-conspirators have been plotting a coup against my reign. Although he refused to name you specifically, there can be no doubt he planned to usurp my throne in your favor. Because of his treasonous crimes, and to secure my throne, I have since named my infant grandnephew, Ivan VI, as my heir and successor, with Count Byron acting as regent until the boy comes of age. There can be no dispute in this matter, and I expect you to greet this announcement with the zeal and benevolence befitting your station. To ensure this, I will be granting the household I have so graciously allowed you to oversee a royal visit in the next few days. Also, I plan to check on my navy and the city I left to your care in my absence. I hope I will have no reason to find fault in your behavior.

Your Sovereign Empress,
Anna R

Handing the letter to Sergei, I turn my attention back to the basket. Hand over my nose, I lift the lid to reveal a bundle of bloody oilcloth. Removing it with careful fingers, I recoil, fighting back a gag at what lies beneath.

The severed head of Artemii Volynskii.

Even as disgusted as I am by it, I still find myself unable to tear my gaze away while Sergei silently reads the letter. The head is grotesque, hardly recognizable except for the familiar port-wine stain on one cheek. The mouth is agape, tongue severed, flesh waxy, and eyes filmed in white. Artemii had been a favorite of my parents, even serving as the Kazan's governor for a time. After Anna took power, she sent him to the army, then eventually made him one of her top three military advisors. No doubt it was his position, rather than any treasonous activities, which caught Byron's ire, as Artemii was a true Russian and vocally opposed to German influence. Staring at what remains of him, I can't help but recall when I saw him last, so long ago in Peter's court. Artemii had been tall with dark hair and eyes, as foreboding as he was handsome. Now, all that's left of the man is a rotting head in a stinking, bloody basket…and for what?

A familiar sickness rolls through me, viciously twisting my stomach and bringing tears to my eyes.

I've witnessed cruelty like this before. My own half-brother had been executed for the same crime. Treason could only be met with such a fate—it is the way of kings. But, somehow, this feels worse. Cruel and unnecessary. Perhaps because Artemii had always been an ally of my family, or maybe because he had not, to my knowledge, been guilty of such a plot. Another gift from her secret investigations, no doubt, with Byron leading the charge. Tortured until he had said whatever they wanted to hear, even knowing the price he would pay for it. Perhaps by that point, death had been a relief. I hope it was. He was a good man who did not deserve such a fate.

Anna's warning is not subtle. She, lost in her own stupor as she is, is still wise enough to know my very existence is a threat against her. And unless I am clever and extremely shrewd, this will be my fate as well.

"This is..." Sergei begins, his tone furious. I cut him off before he can say more. There are too many others present. The empress has eyes and ears everywhere now.

"The cost of treason against the throne. If he was plotting against her, then the empress did what had to be done."

Finally able to control the shaking in my hands, I close the lid and address the servant, who waits anxiously in the doorway.

"Please remove this from the palace. Burn the entire thing away from here. The empress is granting the Winter Palace a visit, and I would have no remnants of a treasonous plot here."

I'll give Artemii a place of honor as soon as I'm able, I reassure myself, knowing anything less than complete subservience now will cost me my head as well.

When I focus on Sergei, I watch as he grapples to control his rage before he forces his features into a neutral expression, then solemnly nods once.

"We have a guest to prepare for, Sergei. Please see to it. I will be in the chapel. Suddenly, I find myself in need of spiritual guidance."

When he bows, I take my leave from him, wishing nothing more than to find comfort in his arms, but knowing I now must tread extra carefully.

The chapel is aglow with the light filtering through the stained glass that flanks the golden iconostasis. It casts a shattered rainbow of color on the floor. It's warm inside, but I find myself shivering anyway as the archbishop approaches me.

"Your Grace," he says, extending a weathered hand for me to hold as he guides me down the aisle. "Have you come for early Mass?"

"No, I'm afraid…I'm quite shaken and in need of counsel."

"Of course." He motions for me to sit. When I do, he takes a seat in the row in front of me. "Tell me your troubles, so the Lord may extend his mercy."

"The empress has discovered a plot against her,

and she thinks I had a hand in it. She's coming to the Winter Palace, and I fear for my safety."

"Have you a reason to fear?"

"I know of no plots against Her Majesty, and I certainly had no part in any of this. I fear over the sake of my blood alone, she will ever see me as a threat—though I am not one."

"It is said only the guilty hold fear in their heart. Perhaps you, even in thought, have entertained such ideas?"

I shake my head, feigning innocence. "I had thought once, long ago, I was fit to rule Russia, but my God has decided differently. I accept that, and I harbor no ill will or intent. Beyond that, I would never harm my nation in such a way. Blood against blood in a feud that would only destroy innocent lives? I could never..."

"I have known you since you were a child. You have never been one to step aside so easily."

"My father, God rest his soul, raised me to be a queen. But that means putting the needs of my people above my own. I have tried, whatever my station, to do so."

"Have you considered retiring to a convent?"

The idea of it appalls me, so much I must force myself to control my expression at his words.

"I have, though I doubt even that would be enough to keep me safe. But I do not know, truly, if God would have me there. Father, do you think I am cursed?"

"Cursed by God? Why would you wonder such a thing? What crime have you committed?"

Eyes widening, he leans forward. If I had only suspected before, I am now certain. He is listening not for God, but for the empress.

"I think it is the curse of my blood—my father's blood. He was a great man, but he was ruthless. Sometimes, he was even cruel. I have lost my family, my title, and even the love of my life. If that is not cursed, I'm not sure what is."

"You are speaking of the man you were intended to marry, yes?"

I almost correct him, but I quickly catch myself. "Yes, of course."

"Perhaps you need to look at what still remains for you."

"What is that? Please tell me, Father. Because I find myself nothing more than a bird in a cage. I have renounced my name, my claim, everything I once had has been stripped from me, yet I am still not free. I cannot marry—the empress would never allow it. I cannot help my people. I cannot even protect my poor nephew, whose only crime is that Romanov blood flows in his veins. I've had to send him away to keep the wolves from his heels. Now, I fear I will be put to death for nothing more than the misfortune of my birth and the greed of those around me. So, tell me, how can I purge myself of this burden? How can I prove my love and support for our empress?"

He leans back, stroking his grey beard with one hand.

"I think you can only prostrate yourself before your God and your queen, be humble, penitent, and meek in all things, and let his great plan for you reveal itself. Have faith, child. All will be as it is supposed to so long as you accept your place."

"Yes, of course. Thank you." Reaching out, I take his hand, "You are such a comfort to me. I cannot imagine what I would do without your wise counsel."

He pats my hand before standing, "Of course. Go now, child, and pray."

I rise, inclining my head to him. The church, it seems, is still in her grasp. Willing to overlook all the bloodshed she's caused, but to what end? What does she possess that they fear losing?

When he leaves, I return to my seat before falling to my knees.

I do not pray for forgiveness, nor for what might have been. Instead, I pray for courage for what I know I must do. The time for my redemption—or my death—will soon be upon us.

Chapter Ten

Despite her threat, it is almost five weeks before Empress Anna arrives in her golden carriage. She's more rotund than I remember, owed, at least in part, to the nightly galas she hosts. Skin pale, she has rouged her cheeks with bright pink while her lips are thin and dry. Her twin raven-black braids frame her face. As she steps from the carriage, her most recent lover, Count Byron, takes her hand and leads her to where my small court waits to greet her. Byron is a large man. In a perfectly curled white wig and tall boots, he is an overindulged lout, his nose long and sloping against his full cheeks. I'd met him only once before, in passing, when he was a young man in my father's court. He'd struck me as weaselly back then. His expression, smug and full of disdain, is the only feature I recognize.

As they approach, my court either curtsies or bows, respectively. Sergei is at my side, with Lady Lia at my back, and a handful of guards and servants gathered around us.

"Your Majesty," I offer formally, trying not to choke on the words. "Welcome to your Winter Palace."

"Yes," she mutters with a sneer. "It's quite... French, isn't it?"

I force a smile, though I know it is not a compliment. "Yes, as you know, my father had a great love of French architecture. He once called this palace his Versailles."

"Perhaps if your father had loved his own country as much as he loved others... Ah, well, no sense dragging all that up now. I assume you know Count Byron?"

I curtsy again. "Count Byron, I'm pleased you could take the time to visit this beautiful city."

"I was here when this place was nothing but a pile of rocks and a dream. I'd not miss seeing it again."

Behind him, another man appears with a bow. His hair is his own, at least, if powdered white and severely receding across his broad forehead. He's older than I remember him being from his time serving as my father's ambassador, but his face is still small and puckered, giving him a perpetually sour appearance.

"Your Grace," he mutters hastily.

"Count Bestuzhev," I greet him warmly. "I thought you'd be busy handling the affairs of Novgorod."

Rumor had it that Byron had sent Bestuzhev

away, fearing for his position in the queen's bed. But Bestuzhev had refused to go quietly, and the two now enjoyed—at best—a contemptuous relationship.

"Yes, well, Her Majesty asked me to take this journey with her to go over a few matters of state."

"Nothing we couldn't have handled without you, of course," Byron interjects.

Bestuzhev frowns. "Of course."

"Still, it is always good to see you. And you, of course, my dear cousin."

At the term, Anna scrunches her nose.

"Your Majesty," I add quickly.

With a flick of her hand, the footmen scurry to bring in her trunks.

"How are things at *my* palace, Princess Elizabeth?"

"I think you will find everything in order and to your liking. I've had the account records set out so you can go over everything, and I've arranged a tour of the shipyard…"

She waves me to a stop.

"Fine. But first, I shall rest. The journey has been long and dull."

"Of course, Lady Lia can show you to the royal apartments."

On cue, Lia steps forward and curtsies.

Anna practically sneers in disgust. "No, I will find it myself. I have brought my own ladies to assist me."

"As you wish, Your Majesty."

Sergei steps forward, addressing Byron. "Count, is there anything you require at present?"

"I'd like to see those purchase receipts."

"Of course," Sergei offers with a sweep of his arm.

The men stride off, Byron offering a flirtatious wink back at Anna, who blushes like a schoolgirl.

I gesture to Anna, bidding her entrance. "Your Majesty, may I walk with you to your rooms? I do have a small matter I'd like to discuss."

She nods, then motions for the ladies who are just exiting the second carriage to walk behind us.

As we make our way up the grand staircase, I offer her an arm, which she takes. By the time we reach the top, she's winded and wheezing, her cheeks badly flushed from the effort.

"I received your letter and your…uh, basket," I begin plainly.

"Oh, and what did you think of your gift?"

Pulling a fan from her pocket, she begins cooling herself with her free hand, her other arm still linked in mine.

"I was shocked, I admit. But you are the empress. Threats against you—no matter how credible—cannot be taken lightly."

"And do you imagine his confession was not credible? Byron himself oversaw the investigation."

"Alas, I cannot say, though I would never impugn Count Byron's honor. I hadn't heard any such whispers from Volynskii, or I would have brought them to you myself. But either way, you acted as a great queen must."

"Were you very close?"

"No," I admit. "He served in my father's cabinet, then in young Peter's after that. But we rarely crossed paths. I did think him to be a good man, but even good men can sometimes do terrible things."

"So true," she muses. "Men cannot be trusted. Not even men so handsome as your Sergei."

Her tone is light, but there's malice in her words.

"He's not mine, Your Majesty. He was a close friend of Charles, the man whom I was intended to marry before his unfortunate passing. On Charles' death bed, Sergei swore to him that he'd look after me, and he's nothing if not a man of his word."

"I assure you, Elizabeth, any man who keeps your company for so long has more in mind than keeping an oath to a dead friend."

I clear my throat, desperate to shift the conversation off Sergei. "I'm sure you are right, Empress. But in response to your other decree, the naming of your heir, of course I offer my support. I have arranged a feast in your honor for tonight, so we may celebrate the declaration properly—and publicly. I do wonder if you have made any provisions should you choose to marry and have a child of your own?"

Her steps falter, and I have to help steady her.

"I am too old for children. As for marriage, why should I?"

"I'm sorry, I'd only heard rumors you and Count Byron were quite in love. I thought perhaps..."

"Yes, Ernst is a delightful companion, though he is already wed. But then, so is Mikhail. Why should I have to choose just one?" Her accompanying laugh is deep and sultry. "I am a widow and a queen at that. I'm finally free to enjoy the company of however many men I wish. Besides, men are such fickle creatures. Best to keep them like bread. Enjoy what you like while they are fresh, but be able to discard them when they get old and crusty."

"That sounds perfectly reasonable to me," I offer with a forced smile. "I only thought you'd be getting pressure from the church—to marry, I mean."

"The church's thoughts on my marriage or the men who attend me are simply not my concern. They do not trust a woman without a man to rule over her. It isn't in their nature to do so. But they also know who keeps their coffers full and their cathedrals safe."

"Of course," I say.

She pauses, turning to face me fully. "Don't tell me, dear cousin, that you're madly in love and want permission to marry?"

The shock of her words must show on my face because she laughs again.

"No? Good." Her tone sours. "You know I could

not allow it in any case. One living male from your father's line is troublesome enough."

"Peter is just a child," I remind her. "And he's being raised by his father in Holstein."

"And Ivan is just an infant. Yet, one day, he will be king. Someday in the future, they will find themselves rivals, just as you and I find ourselves now. And all rivals must eventually be dealt with."

The venom in her expression sends a chill over me.

"I would not be your rival," I say, knowing it's a lie.

"Nor would I choose to be yours. But God has decided that for us, hasn't he? Now, if you'll excuse me," she says as we reach her room.

Releasing her, I step away, watching as the empress and her ladies file inside, closing the door behind them.

No, Anna will not be won over with sweetness and friendship.

She will not be won over at all.

Chapter Eleven

As the feast winds on, seated as I am beside Anna at the head of the table, I cannot help but notice her entire court is made up of Germans. Not a single foreign diplomat, save for my own, are to be seen. The ladies seem afraid to so much as move unless she bids them do so. Even her own counts and dukes speak carefully, paying tribute to her at every opportunity.

After a time, the group grows boisterous with food and drink, and a dozen court jesters perform, most stumbling around in near lunacy. A minstrel plays decidedly inappropriate tunes, which Anna sings along with at the top of her voice. The entire scene feels like something one might expect from a roadside brothel, not a royal ballroom. But I watch Anna closely. Something is tugging at the back of my mind, some sense of wrongness I cannot place. When she lifts a glass of wine, her hand trembles, and as she brings it to her lips, she falters, the crimson liquid spilling down her chin. She wipes it away quickly, gaze searching for any who might have seen, and I avert my eyes before she can catch me staring.

Across from me, Sergei is deep in conversation with Byron, whose wife sits on Sergei's other side. She's quiet, her expression tense, as she stabs at her plate without actually taking a bite. The lady is actually quite lovely, far too young for the man she has wed—not that he shows much interest in her. My gaze slide to Anna, who sits back, her hands clasped together beneath her chin. Sergei laughs at something Byron says, and Anna focuses on him. Her assessment is quizzical at first, but it soon turns into something I can read all too well. A sudden burst of jealousy flaring inside me, I lean forward.

"Sergei, would you do me the honor of a dance?"

"Of course, Princess."

We excuse ourselves, then make our way to the dance floor. Still, Anna watches him like a hawk about to extend its talons to retrieve its prey, making my stomach tie in nervous knots.

"How are you feeling tonight?" Sergei asks, jarring me from my thoughts.

"Anna has come to kill me, of that I am certain."

"For what cause? You have done everything she's asked of you. Even Byron says your accounts are in perfect order, and—"

I cut him off. "Anna told me. She said someday Ivan would have to deal with Peter just as she's going to have to deal with me."

"Perhaps she was just trying to frighten you?"

I blink up at him. "She's been here less than a day, and you are already in her thrall?"

The anger threaded through my voice is impossible to conceal, and he seems surprised by it.

"No, of course not," he offers with a frown.

"Do you imagine her harmless then? Or have you already forgotten the head she delivered to me only a few weeks ago?"

"No, Lizzy, but..."

Perhaps he doesn't see her—truly see her—for what she actually is.

Dangerous.

Still, I know there is one thing I can say to convince him.

"She asked me if I was in love. If I ever hoped to marry. Then she laughed and told me that she'd never allow it even if I were. Too many of my father's descendants alive as it is, she said."

His face falls. My words have done their job.

"What do you plan to do?"

Lowering my voice, I glance at Anna once more before speaking. "I think she's ill. She could hardly walk to her rooms earlier. And have you noticed she just sits there when she could be dancing or joining in? I think there's something wrong with her."

"If the empress is ailing, she'd keep it a closely guarded secret. I doubt anyone outside of her most trusted advisors would know."

I nod. "It would explain her sudden desire to eliminate any threats. She's named a newborn child as her heir. It's a weak position should she die before he comes of age."

"Unless she eliminated any potential rivals first."

"Exactly. Sergei, do you believe me now?"

Gently, he cups my chin in one hand. "I have never doubted you. Not in anything."

"Then we must be sure. We must discover what ails her."

"What do you need me to do?" he asks with a deep sigh.

"Ask her to dance. Perhaps, as loathe as I am to suggest it, you must charm her. Sway her to your confidence."

"If I pursue her, only to turn her away, she will know our true intentions. She is well aware I am your man. She will not trust me unless she thinks I've forsaken you completely."

He's right, of course. Anna is too clever to be fooled by a simple flirtation. He'd have to be close to her…much closer…

Even as I think it, my stomach churns in rebellion.

"You're frowning," he says. "What are you thinking?"

"Only that you're right."

"As much as I love hearing you say that, I wish I weren't."

"You must seduce her. Fully. It is the only way."

He stops, face shocked as he braces me in his arms. "You're serious?"

"I do not like it any more than you do, but it might be the only way."

"You're asking me to sleep with the empress? To begin a relationship with that foul woman?"

Exhaling sharply, I avert my gaze, unable to meet the accusation in his eyes. I can barely stand the shame choking me as it is.

"If it were only myself at risk, I would never ask this of you. But little Peter… he's all I have left."

"Not all. You have me. And I will protect you both, just as I always have."

When I peer up at him, his green eyes swim with sincerity.

"I know you will."

"But this?"

"She will fall completely in love with you, Sergei. How could she not? How could any woman not?"

Shaking his head, he snorts. "You clearly didn't."

"If you believe that, then you do not know me at all."

My words hang in the space between us, heavy and hollow. A blade that slices us both to the quick.

Despite my best efforts, I love Sergei. And yet, I would sacrifice us both if it meant keeping Peter safe. If it meant keeping Russia safe.

"Peter and I will die—and soon. The nation will

dissolve into chaos. Ivan cannot rule, and his so-called regent will be ruled by the Prussian king. The Romanov dynasty will fall, and all of Russia will fall with it."

Sergei is quiet for a long time as he considers my words. Finally, he grins, but it is tinged with so much sadness it cuts me to my very core. "I genuinely believed there wouldn't be anything you could ask of me that I would not do, but I see now there are some lines I will not cross—not even for you. Goodnight, Your Grace."

When he releases me, I nearly stumble. As he cuts through the horde of dancers to exit the ballroom, a familiar voice cuts through the fog in my brain.

"Princess?"

"Oh, Count Bestuzhev."

I wipe at my eyes before turning to him.

"May I have your company for a dance?"

"Of course."

He takes my hand. When we start to sway, he steps on my foot. I wince.

"My apologies, Princess. I have not had a formal dance in some time."

"No balls in Novgorod?"

"No, thankfully. I'm afraid I have not had a mind for frivolities since my exile."

"Exile? I'd heard it was an appointment for the crown?"

He smirks. "I'm afraid I've committed the grievous sin of falling from the empress' good graces."

"Is it her graces you've fallen from, or Count Byron's?" I ask pointedly.

"Most days, they are one and the same. But what of you? How is life at Winter Court? I was here during your mother's reign, brief as it was. She was always so bright. She seemed to bring light to everything around her."

Until she was murdered by the treacherous men seeking to steal her throne, I want to say. But I hold my tongue, forcing myself to be pleasant.

"Mostly quiet. Peaceful."

"So I hear. The city is flourishing while the rest of the nation seems to struggle."

"The empress has been kind with her funding for the city. I have only used those allotments to the best of my ability."

"The people love you for it. But then, the people have always loved you. As they loved your father."

"That is kind of you to say."

"It is simply true."

A commotion at the banquet table catches my attention. Anna is being helped to her feet by Byron. At first, I think it's to dance, but she's hunched forward as he quickly leads her from the room.

"Is the empress unwell?" I ask, filling my voice with concern. "Should I fetch the physician?"

“She brought her own. It’s nothing, I’m sure. She has suffered terribly with gout these past years. Nothing to be concerned with.”

“My father had the same, gout and stones. The pain was excruciating. I could hear him screaming for days on end. I should go see to her.”

He grasps my wrist when I try to pull away.

“I would not.”

“Why not?”

“Because we both know the empress has come to kill you.”

Chapter Twelve

Roughly, I pull away, striding to the exit with Bestuzhev close behind. When I reach the grand staircase, I see Anna pitched forward over the bottom steps, groaning wordlessly. Before I can be spotted, Bestuzhev grabs me and pulls me into an alcove, covering my mouth with his palm.

He whispers, "Do not let them see you. If they know you're here, they will take you right now. You must trust me on this."

Reluctantly, I nod. When he removes his hand, I peer around to watch as one of her guards lifts her and carries her up the stairs.

"That is not gout," I challenge him once they've gone.

"No, it's not."

"Why have you come? Why did you warn me?"

"The empress wants you dead. You know as well as I do that your claim to the throne is stronger than hers—certainly stronger than some infant the court has never even seen. Volynskii was just the beginning. They forced him to confess to a plot to implicate you, so they could have you questioned and eventually beheaded."

Even though I'd thought as much, hearing him say it so plainly drives a chill through me.

"That does not answer my question, Count. Why are you telling me this now?"

"Because I have been removed from court. Replaced. I would have my redemption."

"You mean, you would have your revenge."

"Call it whatever you will. Her time is short, and she knows it. She's already having coins minted with Ivan's image, and transferring lands to Byron to secure his regency. You, and Peter, are the last pieces she must dispose of."

I step out of the alcove, my mind spinning. My time has run out. There is no other option now. I must flee. Sergei can come with me. We'll fetch Peter and abscond, perhaps to France. Surely Louis would protect us.

"You are thinking of running, no doubt."

Pivoting on my heel, I face the man who, as surely as he's breathing, is sealing my death warrant.

"What choice do I have now?"

"She has already sent men to retrieve the young heir."

"She's bringing Ivan here?"

"No, she's bringing Peter."

The blood in my veins turns to ice. My nephew,

the child I could not have, the last piece of my sister, of his namesake, my half-nephew and lover, the last true Romanov. The chill spreading inside me numbs everything else, driving out all warmth until I'm shaking from it.

"What are you offering me, Count?" I ask finally, void of any emotion. "What do you want in exchange for his safety? For my own?"

"Meet me tomorrow at noon, at the place where your parents wed in secret. You know where?"

The nearly hidden chapel behind the St. Petersburg Abbey.

"I do."

"Then I will see you tomorrow."

"Know this, if you betray me, I will point my finger directly toward you during my interrogation. I'm sure Count Byron would be just as happy to see us both lose our heads."

"Till tomorrow then."

He turns to leave, but I stop him by calling out.

"Wait, what do I do tonight?"

He shrugs. "It may be the last night on earth for us both. I suppose you should do whatever you desire most."

He leaves, heading back into the growing noise from the ballroom. I hesitate only a moment before making my way up the stairs.

If I die tomorrow, there is only one place I want to be tonight.

Sergei's chamber door is closed, so I tap gently. When it doesn't open, I let myself inside. I don't know what I expected to find. Perhaps he'd be reading a book in his chair or lounging in bed, half-dressed. Instead, I see him lying in a basin of hot water, a damp cloth covering his face. Closing the door, I silently creep over to him, stripping off my shoes as I go. Stopping short, I reach back and release the ties from my gown. It flutters to the ground at my feet. Hearing the swish of fabric, he jolts upright and uncovers his face.

"Lizzy?"

In only my shift and corset, I kneel beside the tub. I take a sponge in my hand, then wet it before gently stroking his chest.

"What are you doing?"

I smirk. "I'm taking care of you, which is what I should have done earlier. Can you forgive me?"

He doesn't answer. Instead, he only relaxes against the washbasin and lets me bathe him. Finally, I release the sponge, then climb into the tub with him. Water splashes out around us when I press myself against him, kissing him tenderly. With a deep sigh, he pushes me away.

"Lizzy," he begins again, but I silence him with another kiss.

"No, please, Sergei. I don't want to fight. I just want to be here with you tonight."

He shakes his head. "Why? An hour ago, you were pushing me into the empress' bed. What has changed?"

"I think...I think I might die tomorrow. And I'd like to spend my last night with you."

That's all. I want him to soothe me, to make me forget, if only for a little while.

He takes my face between his hands, his eyes searching mine.

"If you honestly believe that, then leave with me. Right now. We can go so far the empress will never find us."

"She has Peter. Sergei, she's bringing him here tomorrow."

"How do you know?"

"Bestuzhev told me."

"And you believe him?"

"I do. He's been removed from court, exiled. He has no reason to lie."

"Unless he's a spy for her. Have you ever considered that?"

"Of course I have. But, either way, I can't leave Peter unprotected. Tomorrow will come, and I will face it. Either my time will end, or it won't, but, right now, all I can do is be here. With you."

Pushing around me, he rises, then steps out of the bath, wrapping his lower body in a linen towel.

"You have to go to Anna right now. Tell her Bestuzhev approached you, trying to convince you to plot against the crown. She'll see that you are no threat to her."

I lick my lips. "No."

"No?"

"No," I repeat. "I will not waste my time trying to win her trust. She's insane, Sergei. She's ill and addled, and nothing I could say or do will convince her otherwise. And I will not cower to that imposter queen for one more second longer."

"Elizabeth, you must be patient."

"I've been patient. For years, I've watched as she's bankrupted my nation, decimated our troops, and washed her hands in the blood of innocent men. But that's done now." I stand, the cloth of my shift heavy around my legs, dripping and cooling the longer I stand here. "All I can do now is fight. I will do whatever it takes to protect the people I love and the nation I was born to lead. Or, so help me, I will die trying."

"I'm begging you, Lizzy, do not do this. Come with me."

"I am with you, Sergei. But I will not run. I'm asking you to stand with me now."

He shakes his head. "And I'm asking you to save yourself. If not for your sake, then for mine. I cannot lose you."

Sitting on the edge of the basin, I sigh, a chill

creeping across my flesh as the water cools.

"Is this to be it then? The great chasm between us that neither can cross?" I ask with a frown. "If so, then we are already lost."

"There must be another way." He paces, raking a hand through his dark hair. "I'll go to Anna now. I'll do as you asked."

"It's too late for that. Anna took ill at dinner, and she retired to her chambers. Hopefully, it will give me the time I need to make my arrangements."

Shoulders slumping, his face falls into a resigned frown.

"What can I do?" he asks after a long silence.

Carefully extricating myself from the tub, I walk to him, curling myself against the warmth of his bare chest.

"You can love and forgive me, one last time. I swear I will not ask for it again."

Without another word, he lowers his chin and wraps his arms around me in a powerful embrace, his lips finding mine quickly and without hesitation. Bending, he sweeps me from my feet, cradling me in his arms as he carries me to his bed.

Chapter THIRTEEN

The dawn comes far too quickly. I watch the rise and fall of Sergei's chest for some time before finally slipping back to my room. Lady Lia paces in my outer chamber, chewing her nails as she does when she's anxious. Upon seeing me, she relaxes, rushing to my side.

"Your Grace, Count Byron has requested you join him for breakfast."

I don't bother hiding my annoyance. "And the empress?"

"The servants are whispering, saying she was having fits all evening. Is the empress ill?"

"I believe so. Likely the same gout and stones my father suffered with, and possibly more beyond that."

"That sort of pain can cause terrible rages, unthinking outbursts. Perhaps, if I may be so bold, you could send one of the clergies to be at her side to offer her some support through this difficult time?"

"To what end?" I ask, recognizing the tone of

conspiracy in her voice.

"Well, if she were to…perhaps reject the priest, or have one of her tantrums in his presence…"

"It could be enough to tarnish her pious image with them," I say, finally understanding her thought process. "Yes. I think that might be a wonderful idea. Also, have the kitchens send up some salted calf liver with a heavy sauce. She will need her strength to battle her affliction."

Of course, it was also the one dish my father always rejected, saying it worsened his pains. But the longer she is ill, the more time I will have to set my plan in motion.

"What else can I do?" she asks.

"Can you get word to Louis, but do so in secret? Tell him what is happening and ask for his support. I know he will give it. As soon as I am on the throne, I will offer an alliance with France."

"I can. Consider it done."

"One last thing—the uniform I wore for our spring gala? Please have it cleaned and pressed, then ready it for me. I think I will soon require it again."

Lia curtsies. "Of course, Your Grace."

She quickly helps me dress before hurrying off to do as I've asked. Once I've prepared, I make my way to the dining room where Byron waits, nibbling on bread and clotted cream while looking through a stack of papers. Seeing me, he stands, bowing at the neck.

"Princess, thank you for joining me."

"Of course. When the empress' most trusted advisor calls, I am happy to answer. What can I do for you today, Count?"

When he motions for me to sit, I do, the servants efficiently filling a cup of coffee for me.

"I must commend your record keeper. Your accounts are all in order and well balanced."

"I will pass along your kind words."

Setting the papers aside, he folds his hands under his chin and gazes at me intently. "May I be blunt, Your Grace?"

"Please do."

"Our ongoing battle with the Ottomans has seriously depleted the royal coffers. Yet, St. Petersburg seems to be thriving. Flourishing even."

"We do what we can for the people of the city," I say simply, unable to avoid the twisting in my gut that warns me of a dark agenda behind his compliment.

"Do you imagine it is right for this one city to be so comfortable while the rest of our nation suffers?"

There it is. The twisting of the knife. If I say no, then my funds vanish. If I say yes, then I'll look spoiled and selfish, thinking only of my own comfort above the suffering of others.

"Let me ask you, Count, do you imagine it is right the nation suffers at all? We fight wars with little gain while our allies are beaten back at every turn. We give more and more land to the nobles, but then make the landlords responsible for their taxes. Perhaps if the empress were to employ a more competent lord to oversee the Royal Purse, such economic hardships could be avoided."

"You think to blame the empress for these hardships?"

"Of course not. I am simply offering the use of our personal accountant for Her Majesty. I'm certain he could look over her own ledgers and offer some suggestions."

Sitting back in his chair, Byron folds his arms across his chest. Behind him, a massive framed portrait of my father hangs. It's one of my favorites—Peter the Great, astride his tall steed, with his sword lifted high. Golden light from above encircles him like a halo. God's own chosen. The man who brought sanity and strength to the nation. I cannot help but think how weak and small Byron looks by comparison. He is not a king. The man isn't even a regent. He's just another sad little man attempting to climb to heights he does not deserve on the backs of his betters.

Before he can speak again, I lean forward, filling my voice with concern.

"How is my dear cousin, Byron? I saw her leave the feast last night, and my lady tells me she was quite ill through the evening. Is there anything I can do to comfort her?"

"Anna is healthy as an ox, I assure you. It's only her gout causing her some mild pains."

I nod. "I am glad to hear it. I'll ask the archbishop to visit her later, to offer the comfort of prayer."

He frowns, but he says nothing.

"If Her Majesty needs rest today, I would be happy to escort you on a tour of the shipyard on her behalf while we wait for her to recover?" I offer, giving him my most pleasant smile.

He seems as if he is about to accept, but then shakes his head. "Thank you, but I should remain close today. In case the empress needs me."

"Of course. She is indeed lucky to have such a devoted friend looking after her."

"Yes, well, I am the lucky one."

His words are soft, and there's a flicker of something in his eyes, an emotion that speaks not of politics and power…but of love. He genuinely loves her. Devotion is a rare and complicated beast. No wonder he hates Bestuzhev so much. He's jealous.

And jealousy is nothing if not exploitable.

"I think it must be hard for Bestuzhev, being so far from her while she's suffering so. When my father had his pains, only my mother's presence could soothe him. Despite his fits, she would stay to stroke his hair and sing to him. I can only imagine how hard it must be watching someone you care for in such misery. That's probably why she asked him to come back now. Just having him close must be a balm for her."

His face twists into a grimace. "She called him back to secure Ivan's position with the nobles, nothing more."

Ah, of course. The nobles are wavering in their support of the child. As they should be. And Byron doesn't have the position to do it himself. For all his maneuvering, he's still just an outsider, a foreign influence. No, the nobles must not appreciate that.

"Of course, you must be right. I should be going, but do give her my love," I say as he stands to leave.

Once he's gone, I make my way to the kitchens, then order a basket of fresh pastries. I head out to the stables, preparing to ride out to the Galley Wharf to greet my subjects.

The breeze from the Neva River is thick and salty, and I inhale deeply as we approach the shipyard fortress. The scent always reminds me of my mother, of how she loved to picnic along the wet banks during the summer while my sister and I played on the grassy berms nearby. Sometimes, Father would join us as well. In those moments, we weren't members of the Great House of Romanov—we were just a happy little family, living a simple, quiet life.

That was the life my mother truly longed for.

Humble and quiet with the people she loved all around her. She never wanted the crown or the endless sacrifices that came with it. That was my Father's idea. He wanted to make her queen. She only wanted to make him a home.

I recall when he'd once rolled up his trousers and waded into the river, picking stones for her to skip across the smooth surface. The way he looked at her—it was like a man staring at the moon, wanting nothing more than to bask in its glow. He loved her, feverishly, from the moment they met, or so he'd once told me. Though he was already wed with a son in the cradle, he set his family aside to marry her in secret. Later, he married her again, formally, in the Grand Cathedral. He put a crown upon her head, much to the dismay of his council, who called her a witch, and worse. They whispered she had entranced him, bewitched the great king. Perhaps they were right, because from that moment on, he looked at no other.

When I was young, it felt like a fairy tale, their romance. Only now can I see it for what it truly was.

The first act in a tragic play, a misstep that would doom us all long after they were gone.

Lady Lia and I wander through the yard, inspecting the small garrisons and handing out treats to the soldiers. She takes notes while I speak to each one, asking about their families and their health. She busies herself with making lists of anything they need or any grievances they have. We tour the foundry where the great gates of the Winter Palace were forged, compliment the craftsmen, and christen the new ships.

It is nearing midday when we return to the palace. Lia and I head straight to my chambers.

"I must go for a bit," I tell her in hushed tones. "If anyone asks, I'm taking a rest from my outing today."

"Yes, Your Grace."

Changing into one of Lia's simple gowns, I tuck my hair under a tall, forest green calash bonnet, then slip through the corridor and to the stables unseen.

"The sun has risen, and I see your head is still attached to your shoulders," Sergei teases, appearing from one of the stalls.

"The day is still young," I bite back.

"Lizzy," he pleads. "Wherever you are going, let me follow. Let me help you."

"Has Peter arrived yet?"

He sighs. "No."

"When he does, do you think you can get spirit him away somewhere safe? The Cathedral, perhaps? They can offer him sanctuary within the walls if it comes to that."

"I will do what I can."

I mount the mare quickly, not glancing back for fear I'll lose my nerve.

"Thank you, Sergei. For everything."

With that, I spur the chestnut to a strong gallop and race from the palace grounds into the woods. It's not far to the old chapel, hidden in the thicket of the forest where the crumbling remains of the St. Ekaterina Church still sit, now ominous and foreboding, overgrown with green vines and moss.

After dismounting, I tie the horse to a nearby tree and stride into the ruins. The roof is mostly gone now, lost to the ravages of time, but the walls remain, carved stone engraved with effigies of the Holy Saints and Apostles. In the center, under the remains of the mosaic dome, Bestuzhev stands, his hands folded in front of him as he stares up into the warm daylight.

"I had thought you might not come," he says, finally turning his gaze to me.

"Afraid I'd forgotten the way?" I ask simply, walking toward him. "Or afraid I'd flee?"

"No, you are far too much like your father for that. He never knew when to run, either."

"What do you mean?" I ask.

He smirks. "When I was young, I once rode on the front with your father. Our first battle against the Turks. Your mother rode with him as well, in armor made for a woman, right by his side. We were surrounded by the enemy, our forces lost, and only a handful of us remained. We were moments from being captured or killed. But your mother went to the Turks in secret, trading her jewels in exchange for them allowing us to retreat. She saved your father's life that day—saved us all. Though if it had been up to your father, I believe he'd have preferred to die in glorious battle."

"Is that why you've come to me now? Some sense of obligation? To repay her for her actions?"

"No, I'm far too old and too callous for that."

"Then, why? What do you have to tell me that must be spoken here, in this place?"

"I'm here to offer you the last of what you need to remove Anna for good."

From his breast pocket, he produces a folded letter and hands it to me. I scanned it. It's a letter between Anna and Byron, discussing seizing funds from the church to fund the war in Azov.

It is beyond damning since it proves Anna has been stealing from the church.

"So you see, now you have it. The support of the nobles, the love of the soldiers, and, with this, the approval of the church. Everything you require to stage your coup."

"Anna is ill, weak from her gout."

"And other ailments. The reason she did not arrive in St. Petersburg as scheduled was that she was recovering from a fit that left her unable to speak for some days."

"That's why she named her heir. Why she is suddenly so interested in removing Peter and me from possible succession. I suspected as much. She called you because the nobles are stirring against her."

"Correct. She needs a diplomat to soothe them."

I stare at him for a moment as a sly grin creeps across his face.

"And what do you gain from this, besides your revenge?" I demand.

"A seat on the council once you reinstate it. I wish to be royal chancellor once more. And…" He hesitates, closing the space between us and trailing a single finger up my arm. "I am quite fond of being the consort of the queen."

"You want me to marry you?" I nearly spit the words, making him chuckle dryly.

"Nothing so pedestrian as that, I assure you. But you are young and beautiful. I would not only like a place at your side, but also in your bed as well."

"You would make me a queen and a whore in the same day?" The venom in my tone is sharp, but he is not put off by it. Instead, he draws closer, so impossibly close I feel the warmth of his breath on my face.

"You will find I have a great deal to offer you in the times to come. My counsel, my support, my loyalty. But I know too well how easily women can be swayed by the men in their beds, and so I want to make sure I'm among them. A queen with one lover is his puppet, but a queen who has many is the master of all."

"I am no man's puppet," I say, beginning to shake with rage.

"Not even your beloved Sergei's? He who has your heart and controls your ear? Would you let him command you? And, through you, your nation? That is what the nobles whisper, you know. That you are his pet. And as good a man as he may be, they tire of empresses who rule under the thumbs of their lovers."

My jaw clenches so tightly I have to speak through my teeth. "No."

"Then, my beautiful princess, this is the price. For your crown, your life, and young Peter's life. The only question is—are you willing to pay it?"

His question rings in my ears. My thoughts come quickly, in a torrent. What would my father do? My mother? What would they sacrifice on the altar of Russia?

At that moment, I'm no longer Lizzy. No longer the frightened child who stoically watched her brother's execution. No longer the innocent girl swept up in the glamour of Versailles and its handsome king. No longer the naïve young woman who thought to trade her title for a safe, quiet marriage to a minor noble.

I'm only Elizabeth, rightful empress, daughter of Peter the Great.

The true Romanov heir.

I lean forward until my lips nearly touch his, and

he sucks in a surprised gasp. Reaching behind me, I begin unlacing my dress. The choice is unspoken, but it has already been made. Whatever the price, I will pay it. Holding his eyes, I call forward all the strength in my blood and reply simply, but firmly, as I release my gown to the floor at my feet.

"Yes."

Chapter FOURTEEN

My ride back to the palace is slow, painfully so. My body aches, my mind tormented by the choice I've made. But there is no room for regret now. No sorrow for what might have been. My mother may have wished for a humble, quiet life, but that was never my destiny. I was born to rule. It is as much a part of me as the blood in my veins. Never have I felt so singular of purpose, so focused. So I ride back to the palace, my back straight, head high, not bothering to conceal myself. I know Sergei will not forgive me for this. How could he? How could I even ask it of him? I have irrevocably severed us.

And I would do it again.

He's not in the stable when I arrive. It's a small comfort not having to face him so soon, but the moment I step inside the palace, the servants buzz with whispers.

"What has happened?" I demand, grabbing the footman nearest me.

He bows quickly, his young cheeks flushed.

"The empress," he says, his voice shaking. "She's dead."

Wasting no time, I rush up the stairs to the hall outside her chamber. The archbishop stands silently by her door. Seeing me, he nods.

"I've given the empress her last rights. There's nothing more that can be done. She's been called home to her Lord."

I face him, pulling the letter from my pocket, then handing it to him. He skims it, his face paling.

"Will you support me?" I ask firmly.

He stammers, but he does not answer.

"The time has come. There can be no question," I urge.

"It is in the hands of God," he says finally. "But I believe you are fulfilling God's plan. If you are victorious and no blood is shed, we will support you."

"I swear no lives will be lost this day, not by my hand or at my order. I swear my rule will see an end to the recent bloodlust and madness that has gripped this nation over these past years."

Taking the silver cross from around his neck, he holds it out to me. "Take this, and the others will know the church stands with you." Then he reaches out, laying a hand on my head. "Go with God, my child."

I nod once, then enter her chamber. The physician sits in the corner, cleaning his tools. Beside the bed, Byron kneels, his head on the bed beside

Anna's pale face. I walk to her other side, then lay a hand on hers. It's already cooling, the life gone from her eyes.

"May you find peace and mercy in the arms of our Father," I whisper before gently closing her eyes.

At my words, Byron looks up. Only then do I realize his wife is standing behind him, crying softly.

Byron stands, shouting.

"The queen is dead. Long live King Ivan."

The room falls into silence around us as I motion to the page.

"Ring the bells for our fallen empress." Then, turning to my guard, I continue. "You, Take Count Byron and his wife to the chapel and keep them there. No one is to see them or speak to them, and they are not to leave. Understand?"

He bows, lowering his rifle at the shocked count.

"What…what are you doing?" Byron demands. "I am regent here. It has been declared."

Lowering my chin, I glare at him.

"Tell me, faithful guards, who do you serve? This foreign usurper, this creature who has traded the soul of our nation for gold and power? Who has sent your brothers-in-arms to meaningless deaths for the sake of his own pride? Or will you serve me, the daughter of Peter the Great, the true heir to my father's throne?"

Behind me, their voices are loud and robust. "We stand with the true empress. Long live the queen!"

Byron takes an unsteady step back.

"You came to kill me, to destroy my family, to usurp my crown. If you thought me dangerous before, then you will want to watch me over the next days very carefully. Now go and pray. Pray for mercy because you will find none here."

With that, I sweep from the room. Sergei rushes to greet me in the hall, striding to keep up with me as I head to my chamber. Throwing the doors open, I call Lady Lia.

"It's time. Quickly, help me change."

"Is it true? Anna is dead?"

"It is," I answer as Sergei prepares my sword. "Has Peter arrived yet?"

"Not yet, though they expect him soon."

"He must be protected at all costs. Send the palace guard to ride out to meet them on the road. They must take possession of him before our enemies can."

"Of course."

"And, Sergei, go prepare the horses. Get word to Bestuzhev. I want you both riding at my side today. Send out the call to the regiment, tell them their true empress is coming to greet them."

With a frown, Sergei bows and makes his hasty exit. Lia finishes dressing me, and I take her hand.

"I need you to find the French ambassador Anna sent away. Have him brought here, to St. Petersburg, as soon as possible. And gather the other nobles. I want to see them tonight."

She nods nervously. "I've already sent a messenger to my king. He will have word before the day is out."

"Thank you, Lia. We must move quickly before Anna's German allies can rally against us."

"Of course."

Sergei and Bestuzhev wait for me in the foyer, both looking uneasy.

"My most trusted general and my new chancellor, come. Let's make haste. We must take the garrison to Brunswick to secure Ivan and his mother."

We ride to the guard quarters first, where they mount and join us. Then, we head to the regimental headquarters, where the other soldiers are gathered. Preobrazhensky Regiment stands, their swords raised, red uniforms polished and gleaming as if for inspection as we approach. Taking the lead, I ride up to their line.

"The Empress Anna is dead. Now it is you, brave warriors, who must decide the fate of Russia. Will you stand with those who have stolen my inheritance and would crush our brave nation? Or will you stand with me, the daughter of the king and the one true ruler of Russia?"

Row by row, each soldier drops to one knee, their hands over their hearts as they pledge themselves to me with a thunderous cheer.

"Then gather your weapons. It is time to secure

the throne. For Russia!"

They cheer again, then gather their arms.

With my army at my back, we ride through the night without stopping, arriving at the home of the infant Ivan and his mother at sunrise. Only one man stands between us, Lieutenant Colonel Count von Munnich. The lone guard still loyal to Anna raises his sword. My officers capture him quickly, then drag him away.

"Do not kill him," I order loudly. "God has ordained that no blood be spilled this day."

They obey, shackling the man and forcing him to his knees as we dismount and make our way into the courtyard. A few more men wait within, not soldiers, but foreign nobles, Germans sent to look after the household. I raise my silver cross high.

"I have been chosen by Russia and God to secure the throne. Kneel before me now or face the wrath of both."

The servants kneel first, followed quickly by the few clergies, and, finally, the nobles.

"Bring me the child and his mother," I order Sergei. "But do not harm them."

He nods once, then strides inside while I address the others.

"The false empress is dead, and Russia has spoken. We will not submit to rule by unworthy men. By the will of my father and the grace of God, I have come to claim what is rightfully mine. You plotters, you foreign usurpers, you who have spilled the blood of my people, you are all banished from this land. The child Ivan is declared Damnatio memoriae. He never was, and never will be, emperor. His claim is invalidated by blood, by oath, and by the will of God Almighty. If any speak otherwise, their tongues will be ripped from their head and their bodies imprisoned in Siberia for the rest of their days." I lift my sword—my father's sword—over my head. "I am Empress Elizabeth, daughter of Peter the Great, and I am Russia!"

The men around me cheer, the sound deafening. Sergei leads the family out, the babe swaddled in his crying mother's arms. Beside them, a nursemaid sobs.

"Please don't hurt the child," the nurse calls out. I march across the field, stopping short of the mother, who says nothing but beseeches me with desperate eyes.

"Give him to me now, and I swear to you that no harm will come to him," I offer gently.

"What will you do with him? With us?" she asks, her voice shaking.

"No more or less than what was done to me. He will be stripped of his title, of his name, and of his inheritance. But he will live. That is my oath."

Finally, with a single kiss on his tiny forehead, she places the babe in my arms.

I look down at him, his eyes droopy and his

cheeks full and round. But I do not see a child. I only see my enemy.

Mounting my horse, I order them to bring the mother and nurse as we ride back to the palace. The sun shines upon us as we parade ourselves through the square. All around us, people come out to cheer.

I know they are calling my name, shouting blessings, but the words are drowned out by the now-wailing bundle in my arms.

Chapter Fifteen

By the time we return, night has fallen, and the candles are lit around the palace. The infant and his family have been taken to the nursery under heavy guard until I can decide what to do with them. I'm weary into my very bones as I sit in my private office, joined by Sergei and Bestuzhev. Counts Durgalov, von Munnich, and Lowenwolde—Anna's inner circle of advisors—and Count Byron join us, too, except they are in shackles before me.

"You cannot do this." Byron begins his tirade once more, his face twisted with rage.

The others remain silent, seeming to accept their fate. Of course, none watched the regency they were promised being torn from their fingertips.

"I can, and I have," I say simply, trying to keep the exhaustion from my voice.

"If you think I'm going to bow to some illegitimate whore—"

Before Byron can say another word, Sergei backhands him with such force he falls from his chair and onto the floor with a whimper.

"Russia has spoken. Her people tire of groaning under the weight of your supposed rule, but I have delivered them from your degrading foreign oppression. It was the corrupt council Anna herself dismantled that began this farce, and I have come to end it. I will deliver my nation from your foul policies and false leaderships. By birth and by blood and by the support of the people, I am the true empress."

"What do you want from us, then?" Durgalov speaks up.

"Nothing. For you possess nothing. From this moment on, all your lands, all your serfs, all your personal possessions, are forfeit to the crown. It will not be enough to replenish our coffers, but it will begin to repay the balance with which you have left us. In addition, Counts von Munnich and Lowenwolde, along with their families, will immediately be exiled to Siberia."

"But you, Count Durgalov, once a friend of my father's, for having plotted against my mother and me, for abandoning your oath to the House of Romanov and its rightful heirs, you will be broken on the wheel. And then, once your heart is contrite, you will be beheaded."

He slumps forward in his chair, his grey wig falling into his lap.

"Please, Empress. I beg for mercy."

"By all means then, beg," I say flatly.

Then, I address Byron, who sits at Sergei's feet, refusing to stand.

"And you, who plotted to kill not only me, but also my nephew. You, who stole from the crown and the church to fund your own depraved amusements, you will have your hands and your tongue removed, so you may never again spread lies or stab anyone in the back. Afterward, you will be flogged. If you survive all that, I will turn you onto the street as a penniless beggar for the people to do with as they will."

He only moans. The guards lift him to his feet, carrying him and the others away. Once they are gone, only Sergei and Bestuzhev remain.

They take the empty chairs across from me.

"Chancellor," I say to Bestuzhev. "I trust you can make the arrangements for my coronation?"

"It would be my honor."

"See to it that every Russian noble is summoned for my presentation. And any of our allies who escaped or were imprisoned by Anna are to be brought home immediately."

"Yes, Your Majesty."

"What will you do with the child?" Sergei asks gently.

Sitting back in my chair, I chew on the end of my quill. "I do not know."

"But you will not kill him?"

"No."

"If I may," Bestuzhev interrupts. "So long as he lives, your enemies will rally around him. They'll seek to use him against you. If he lives…"

I raise my hand. "I will not murder a child. I am not Anna."

My words are firm and unwavering. He nods.

"Perhaps exile the child back to Courtland. He could be anonymously placed with a family there. An orphan with no name and no title. Too far to be a threat, but close enough to keep an eye on him as he grows to manhood."

I rub my eyes. "Yes, I think that is a fair solution."

Sergei seems relieved.

"Also, Peter has arrived. I had him placed in a secure chamber with his nurse immediately."

"Excellent. I will see him before I go to bed."

The men bow. I brush past them, too tired for anything else. My soul is heavy, but my mind is clear. I walk to the room, then wave off the guards who let me enter.

Peter sits cross-legged on the floor, a mop of golden hair in his eyes as he plays with a wooden horse.

"Peter?" I say softly, kneeling beside him. He stands, then bows.

I pull him into my arms. "My little baby, you're getting so big now."

He hugs me back for only a moment before

pulling away.

"Have you come to play with me, Auntie?"

His voice is still childlike, his blue eyes wide and hopeful. He looks so much like my lost love, the Peter who came before him, a king who was taken far too soon. The burden he carried, the burden I now carry, will fall on this Peter's shoulders someday.

A wail from the nursery echoes through the walls, and Peter covers his ears with his fists.

"It's just terrible, Auntie. It has been making that sound for hours. Can't you make it stop? Can't you send it away?"

An image plays through my head. Peter as a man, strong and kind, the crown on his head as the entirety of Russia cheers for him. Then, I see Ivan lurking in the shadows behind him, knife in hand, ready to strike. I shake the vision from my mind.

Eventually, the crying stops. Peter returns to his toys. After I kiss him gently on the head, I ruffle his hair.

"Yes, my little love, I'll make it stop."

Chapter Sixteen

The next weeks come and go in a haze of meetings and paperwork. The Marquis de La Chétardie, the French ambassador, as well as others from Sweden, Poland, and even China, arrive for my coronation.

As I'm going over the final menu for the feast, the marquis approaches me with a formal bow.

"Your Highness," he offers, his French accent thick like honey. "May I speak with you for a moment?"

"Of course," I reply, handing my list off to the cook. "What is it?"

"It is a matter of much delicacy, I'm afraid. King Louis sends his regards, as well as his apologies."

"Apologies for what?"

"I'm afraid he has requested the Lady Lia de Beaumont be returned to his court."

"Oh," I say, taken aback by the request. "Lady Lia is a valued member of my court. Can you tell me why she is so urgently needed in Versailles?"

"Only that she is needed for another assignment."

"Well, I will go speak with Lady Lia on the matter and get back to you. I'm sure you understand my wanting to have her close for this important event."

"Yes, the coronation. Of course. Shall I tell the king to expect her soon after?"

"I'll tell him myself, thank you."

As he bows, Sergei enters the chamber. Once the marquis has gone, I relay the request to Sergei, who frowns.

"The timing seems a bit odd, doesn't it?" he asks. He offers me his arm, which I accept.

"It does, but it's not terribly surprising. Lia serves at the behest of her king. I cannot ask her to do otherwise. Even as much as I might wish I could."

"You are Russia's empress, not even Louis would stand against you if you demanded she stay."

"Perhaps, but I will leave it to her to decide."

"That is probably for the best."

"Tell me, is Peter safely back in Holstein?"

"He is," Sergei assures me. "And is Ivan on his way to his new home yet?"

I clear my throat. For days, I've been dreading having to tell Sergei I've changed my mind about the child.

"No. I've decided to move him to a more secure location."

"What location?"

"I've decided to send the child and his remaining

family to the fortress of Dünamünde."

He pivots, cutting off my steps. "Prison? You're sending an infant to prison?"

"I will make them as comfortable as possible, but I cannot risk someone discovering him and secreting him away in the night."

"He's a child."

"He's a weapon. One who can be used against Peter and me. Against everything the Romanovs have built. I cannot risk having it all undone by some rebel supporters. I will not."

"Lizzy," he begins, but I stop him.

"I am not Lizzy. I am Empress Elizabeth. You forget yourself," I snap.

"Empress," he concedes.

"I'm sorry, Sergei, truly. But my mind is made up. I will protect what I have left at all cost."

His frown is severe, but he stays quiet and returns to my side as we walk on.

"Now," I continue. "How goes the treaty negotiations?"

"Bestuzhev is handling the final details. I suspect a treaty will be ready in a matter of days. I must say, much as I dislike him, he is a skilled negotiator."

I sigh, remembering the bargain I'd struck with him. "He is that."

He stops again, this time leading me into a shallow alcove.

He brushes the side of my face with tender

fingertips.

"I've missed you," he whispers.

"Sergei," I murmur, my eyes fluttering closed.

I know I have to tell him about Bestuzhev—about the bargain I made with him—but before I can speak another word, Sergei's lips are on mine, driving any rational thought from my mind.

It's replaced by another, much softer voice, which wonders if perhaps I could have him just one last time…

"No," I say firmly, pushing him back. "I cannot."

He looks stunned, as if I've struck him.

"Sergei, I have to tell you something. Bestuzhev's alliance came at a great cost. He and the other nobles feared that because of our…relationship, you would come to power through me. That I would become nothing more than a pawn or puppet as Anna was to Byron."

He shakes his head, his brow furrowing. "That's ridiculous."

"It is a fear they take very seriously, and with good reason. Bestuzhev offered his support on two conditions—that I keep him as chancellor, and…" I hesitate, having to force the words from my mouth. "That I offer no man exclusive access to my bed."

Sergei steps back, his confusion evident. "And how, exactly, do they plan to enforce this condition?"

"I had to promise to take other lovers, starting with Bestuzhev."

So many emotions flash across his face. I can't tell if he's hurt, angry, sad, or a combination of them all. But when he retreats again, he lets go of my waist as if his hands had been holding hot coals.

"You agreed?" He speaks slowly as if he cannot believe the words he utters.

"I did." I hold my chin high, refusing to allow my sorrow to wash over me.

"And you took him to your bed?" He sounds thoroughly appalled. Disgusted.

While not entirely accurate, I decide to at least spare him the details.

"I have."

"And others?"

"No. Not yet."

"But you intend to?"

"Yes. I must. Publicly and before the coronation. The nobles must have their assurances," I begin, but he finishes for me.

"That you are not in love with me."

I swallow the lump forming in my throat. "Yes."

When he meets my eyes once again, his hold grief in their emerald depths. Grief I know all too well.

I've broken him.

Even knowing what I've done, I feel no regret, only pain. A gaping wound I know will fester between us for the rest of time.

Just when I'm sure he will never speak to me

again, he wipes a hand down his face.

"So that was the price you had to pay to win your crown—to secure everything you've ever genuinely wanted. I only hope it was worth it, Empress." His voice lowers to a hollow, pleading whisper. "Promise me you'll make it worth it."

"I will," I swear.

Turning away from me, he leaves without a backward glance. Somewhere deep inside my chest, the last withered remains of my heart die a bit more with every step he takes away from me.

That evening's feast marks the end of so many eras, that even though I try to enjoy myself, I feel somewhat rudderless instead. My course is set now, the stars have guided me here, so why can't I climb free of this wallowing pit of misery I now find myself in?

The archbishop has sent a gift, and his church choir sings for me as I watch without paying much mind. From my left, Bestuzhev stares my way until he finally lowers his head to whisper to me.

"The coronation is in a few days. You still have one thing you must do to satisfy our arrangement."

His words are like throwing ice water on an already-frozen river.

"If you think you're climbing into my bed tonight,

then you're going to be disappointed," I inform flatly. "We wouldn't want the nobles to think you were bending my ear, now would we?"

He snorts. "Then choose someone. No one with political alliances, though, of course."

"Should I bed the stable boy, then?" I challenge, then down my entire glass of wine.

He scans the room, appraising the candidates.

And I loathe him for it.

"Perhaps we could go round up the guards. Allow you to choose from one of them," Sergei chimes in from where he sits, not even glancing in my direction as he sneers in disgust.

His words are like knives slicing into my chest.

"If that is what she prefers. She does seem to have a soft spot for lowly soldiers, after all," Bestuzhev challenges, leveling a glare at Sergei.

"Enough, the both of you," I demand, feeling a flush of rage creep into my cheeks.

I rise, leaving them with a huff. Wandering around the room, I try to control my anger while pleasantly chatting with my guests.

Why does this have to be so complicated? Kings have been taking lovers for centuries—married or otherwise—and no one ever thinks less of them for it. No one worries about the influence their rendezvous might have over their decisions.

But because I'm a woman, I'm weak. Prey to any man who may catch my attention.

Pathetic.

Of course, I could do what Anna did. Simply make whatever shallow promises I must, then turn my back on them at the next opportunity.

I dismiss the idea as quickly as it comes. No, I am not Anna. I will not be so shortsighted. A queen needs a council to rule effectively, and I need the nobles to trust me and any decisions I make. I would not have them questioning my own mind at every turn.

The bargain must be met.

I spot Lady Lia chatting with some of the singers who are enjoying a glass of wine after their performance, so I join her. They bow, smiling as they introduce themselves.

"Alexei Grigoriev, Your Grace," the last one says, his voice deep, his smile full and genuine.

"You have a lovely voice, Alexis," I offer pleasantly.

His grin increases, and I notice his green eyes holding mine intently. His hair is dark, his brows thick. Cleanshaven as he is, he reminds me a bit of Sergei when he was younger, before the pressures of our relationship had strained him so terribly. No, Alexei looks like a man without a care in the world.

"And you are the most beautiful creature I have ever laid eyes upon," he says in return.

"And a flirt as well," I tease, and he blushes. "Tell me about yourself."

He bows again. "I am a simple serf, Your Majesty.

I was born on a farm near Chernihiv."

"Then I am glad you are here. Your talents would be wasted on a farm, I think."

"You are too kind."

"Though clearly all that time working the land certainly did wonders for your physique," Lia adds, then takes a sip of her wine.

When I raise an eyebrow at her, she smirks over the rim of her glass. Even knowing what she's doing, I'm torn between gratitude and wanting to strangle her. Still, she has a point. He is nicely built, and he has a lovely voice. And, best of all, he's a nobody. A peasant. A Cassock peasant at that.

"Tell me, Alexei, would you be willing to sing for me tonight? Privately? I would love to hear your voice in a more intimate setting." When I bat my eyelashes at him, he grins so widely I think he might strain something.

"Of course, it would be my honor."

"Excellent. I'll see you later tonight."

The matter all but done, I leave him to chat with Lia before making my way back to the table.

"If my lords and ladies would excuse me, I think I'm going to retire. I do have some things to attend to before my coronation."

Sergei shoots me a scowl bordering on disdain, but Bestuzhev beams.

Feeling sick, I head for my chamber and bathe before settling into my most elegant evening dress.

Lady Lia brings Alexei up soon after, showing him in before making her exit for the evening.

"Your Majesty," he says with a bow. "I have come to sing, as you requested."

I wave him in, then settle him on the lounge across from me. He's clearly nervous by the way his eyes dart around. He fidgets with his hands, seemingly at a loss at what he should do.

"Would you like something to drink?" I ask, motioning to the tray Lia has laid out for us.

"Tea, if you have it," he says.

Smiling, I pour him a cup of tea before filling a glass of vodka for myself.

It's warm, burning my throat and belly even as it calms my nerves.

"I must admit, as lovely as your voice is, I have another reason for inviting you here this evening," I offer shyly.

He grins, setting his lute at his feet. "And I must admit I had hoped that was the case."

Rising, I begin to unlace the front of my robe. He jumps to his feet before I can finish.

"Please, Your Majesty, allow me."

After stripping off his tunic in slow, fluid motions, he reaches out, catching me around the waist and pulling me close. I watch his face as he tugs the ribbons free of their bows, then slides his hands up my arms to my shoulders, where he brushes the fabric free. When he lowers his lips to my collar,

I squeeze my eyes closed as I did with Bestuzhev. Holding my breath, I imagine Sergei's hands on my body, his lips dancing across my flesh.

"Are you imagining me to be someone else?" he whispers, making my eyes fly open.

I stammer, but he only smiles. "It's all right if you are. I'll make you forget about him soon enough," he promises, falling to his knees.

Chapter Seventeen

Alexei is as good as his word, so much that I keep him in my chambers for most of the next few days. When I finally emerge, releasing him to return home, I finally feel the weight of my guilt easing from my shoulders. Even Sergei's frown cannot spoil my mood.

"Ah, so you survived. I was beginning to wonder," Sergei says, his voice tense.

"I did what had to be done. It was not such a terrible thing, actually. I believe there is something to be said for enjoying myself without forming an attachment of the heart. Lord knows you men seem to do it easily enough."

"Pleasure without love is just that," he says, clearly choosing his words carefully. "But there is no depth to it."

"There is depth enough in other things," I say flatly. "I, for one, will drown no longer, even as pleasant as it was to drown myself in you." Facing him fully, I continue. "I am sorry, Sergei. Truly. I never meant to hurt you."

"Then you haven't," he says, though his eyes suggest otherwise. "I am alive. You are alive. Peter is alive. Soon, you'll have your crown. It is for the best. I have only wanted you to have what you wanted."

"And I have always wanted you," I admit.

"But as you once said—to be wanted and to be needed are two vastly different things. You always told me you could not love me. You were honest about that. So how could I fault you now? It was my own foolishness to wish for more. I know it can never be, but I will remain your loyal servant. Always."

I want to reach out, to touch him, but something stops me.

"Thank you for that," I say. "I do not think I could do this without you."

Shifting forward, he changes the subject.

"The plans for the coronation are complete. We are sending the servants to Moscow today to make the final preparations for your arrival. Louis has sent someone he hopes you will see fit to add to your new council. Count Armand Lestocq."

"I will greet him in my office."

"There is one last matter," he says, leading me into the library where a bag of gold sits on the closest desk. Plucking one out, he shows it to me. They are the coins Anna had minted in Ivan's image.

"Unfortunately, some were accidentally

distributed before we could stop them."

Taking one, I roll it between my fingers. I can't help but wonder if I'll ever truly be free of the stain of Anna and this child. Or if I'll always be whispered about behind closed doors. An illegitimate heir forced to take the throne by a coup. Are these actions destined to haunt me all my life?

"Have the lost coins found and brought back. I want every last one melted down and reforged," I decide, tossing the coin on the table.

Chapter Eighteen

Lady Lia and a handful of other ladies help prepare me for my coronation. The procession will be long—two days from St. Petersburg to Moscow, where we will proceed through the red gates and to the Dormition Cathedral for the ceremony.

"Have you decided who will crown you?" Lia asks, busily curling my long hair.

"I will crown myself. There is no one else alive fit for the task."

It seems like only yesterday I walked behind Peter, watching him become a king with each step until I finally lifted the crown onto his head.

Despite his promise, he'd failed to keep it there.

I will not make the same mistake.

"Has that been done before?" she asks in hushed tones.

"Never. But all traditions must begin somewhere."

"What better place than with you?" she offers, giving me a soft hug.

"Oh, Lia, are you certain you must return to

Paris? I cannot imagine not having you by my side."

She grins. "I'm sure you'll manage, Empress. But my king calls, so I must go."

"And will you...that is, do you think he will allow you to continue as yourself?"

She frowns. "I do not know. I pray he will."

"Should you ever require a friend in Russia, do not hesitate to call upon me," I say, squeezing her hand.

The maids help me into my gown as the ladies watch eagerly. It's heavy, with full skirts far too large to fit on horseback. I had imagined marching into Moscow in full armor, taking the crown as a warrior with a sword in my hand. Yet, Bestuzhev had convinced me to opt for a less threatening entrance.

After all, I have not come to conquer. I have come to save.

I sit alone in my carriage as the procession begins. My corset is so tight I can hardly breathe, but I force myself to sit gracefully, smiling and waving to those who gather to watch me ride past.

All around me, the world shifts, the solid ground from beneath my feet gone. Today should be a day of victory—for I've finally won the ultimate battle. Instead, I only feel utterly, painfully alone. Everything I've done, every loss, every sacrifice, has been for this day.

Sergei's words echo inside my mind. *I hope it was worth it.*

I squeeze my eyes closed, forcing his voice away. Sergei had decided to stay in the palace—to remain as my general, my guard, and my friend. But he no longer comes to me as he once did, and he no longer looks upon me as he once had. Whatever bond we shared has been truly severed, and I know it's for the best. Someday, I hope he will know love again. He deserves that. But I can no longer afford the luxury of that emotion. Love is a weakness and an uncertainty, and I can afford neither.

It takes days to reach the cathedral. My ladies help me freshen up before I march inside. Remaining stoic as the priests bless and anoint me, I kneel before the altar, surrounded by the icons of gods and prophets and kings, then recite the ancient oath. The priest lifts the crown high upon its velvet pillow, blessing it. Rising, I take it with steady hands, staring at my reflection in the massive red ruby at the top. I can almost see them—my mother and father, my Peter, all those who have ruled before me stretching back generations—all standing behind me. My family. My dynasty.

Lifting the crown, I place it upon my own head before turning to face the assembly.

I am not alone.

I am not afraid.

I am a Romanov.

And I am Russia's queen.

Epilogue

FIVE YEARS LATER

The halls of the palace are eerily silent, even the servants who scurry around to light the evening lamps move as quietly as mice as I sit at my desk, waiting for news.

"The girl should have been here by now," I grumble, impatiently tapping my fingers.

Bestuzhev sits back, folding his arms. "Leave it to the Prussians to be late for every occasion."

I offer him a withering glare, but say nothing.

"I still don't understand why you are so set on this match. You were the one who drove the Germans from court to begin with."

Sighing, I rub the bridge of my nose. We've had this discussion before. As much as I don't want to have it again, I know he isn't going to let the matter drop.

"She is the niece of the man I was supposed to marry. Charles and his family were good people with strong characters. Lord knows we're going to need someone who can handle Peter."

He snorts. "Perhaps if you didn't spoil the boy so—"

"He's not a boy. He's nearly a man, more than ready for a wife and children."

"He's petulant."

Bestuzhev has a point, though I am loathed to admit it. Between Peter's neglectful father and his isolation during the upheaval of Anna's reign, the boy is a bit tender of mind. "He just needs someone with a firm hand and a tender heart. Someone who can guide him."

"He has us for that."

I cannot help but roll my eyes at that. "Yes, because you two are so close. Peter detests you. Hell, he detests me most of the time now."

"The boy drools after King Frederick like he's God made flesh."

"That's his father's influence," I admit. "Another reason the Prussian girl might be a feasible solution. She is German enough to keep him happy, but mayhap I can make a true Russian out of her."

"She'll have to convert to the church."

"I am aware of that. My mother did the same… or have you forgotten?"

That finally silences him, and we wait a bit longer. Just as I rise to stare out the window, Sergei enters, his boots muddy and his cheeks flushed.

"Where have you been?" I demand.

"I went to meet the princess' carriage. And it's a

good thing I did. She and her mother had been set upon by thieves."

I suck in a sharp gasp. "Is the girl unharmed?"

Falling into a chair, Sergei crosses his legs, raking a hand through his dark hair as he grins. "Oh, yes. The girl was quite fierce. Even took on a few of the bandits herself."

"Really?" I ask, my curiosity piqued.

"How very crude," Bestuzhev adds.

"You should have seen her, Elizabeth, truly."

"Where is she?" Bestuzhev demands. "Why has she not come to greet her empress?"

"She was quite soiled from the event. Her gowns were ruined. Poor thing had to travel back in nothing but her slip."

"How completely unsuitable."

I wave off Bestuzhev's comments. "Thank you for seeing to her safety, Sergei. But I must ask, do we have reason to think it may have been more than coincidence they were attacked?"

Sergei leans forward. "We've not had bandits on that road in decades. I doubt it was anything other than an assassination attempt."

Bestuzhev prickles. "Preposterous. No one would dare."

"The Austrian supporters might," Sergei says, leveling an accusing glare at Bestuzhev. "If they were trying to sabotage the Prussian alliance."

"The only one trying to sabotage the alliance is

Prussia itself. They don't want to be our allies—they never have. They mean to rule us."

I sit on the edge of my desk. The timing of the attack could not have been worse. Sergei has a point about that.

"We must be sure the girl is protected. If anything happens to her while she's on Russian soil, King Frederick will use it as an excuse to escalate hostilities, and we cannot afford an outright war when we are already stretched so thin. Sergei, I want you to act as her personal guard. Watch her closely. If you see any indication she or her mother are working against our interests, I want to know immediately."

"Of course."

"Bestuzhev, go and have the seamstress begin making some gowns for our little warrior princess. She will need them as soon as possible. I want her presented to Peter and me tomorrow."

"And the Austrian girl?"

"She should still come as well," I decide. "Then Peter may indicate a fondness for one or the other."

He rises, then bows, leaving me alone with Sergei.

"Truly, you should have seen the girl. Standing in the snow and mud, knife in hand, looking like an avenging angel. I wish Peter could have seen it. He'd have fallen at her feet immediately," Sergei says with a smile.

It's something I haven't seen him do in some time.

"You're impressed with her."

"I am. You will be, too."

"Is she as lovely as they say?"

"She is quite striking."

"And clever?"

He nods. "Her mind seems quite sharp. She actually reminds me quite a bit of you when we first met."

"How so?"

"She has this way of examining you, as if she's picking apart every detail, absorbing her situation at each moment."

"Ah," I say, leaning forward. "You're taken with her."

He shakes his head "I'm intrigued by her is all."

"That's all well and good…as long as you remember she's here for Peter. I would not have her *distracted* by other attentions."

"Please, you know I would never. She's practically a child."

"She's as much a woman as I was when we first met. And for all your years, you're not so old as to be immune to such charms."

"You should know me better."

"I do know you, which is why I'm saying it now-and clearly—so there can be no misunderstandings. I know how you love to rush in and play hero, and I know how you love to take broken birds and mend them. But this is not just a girl—as I was never just a girl. One day, she may be the queen. And you know how dangerous such relationships can become."

He opens his mouth as if to speak, but he closes it instead, a tick working in his jaw.

"What?" I demand. "What do you wish to say to me that you restrain yourself so?"

He shakes his head. "I was only thinking about how much you've changed from those days in the Summer Palace."

"That was always your dream, Sergei. It was never mine," I challenge him.

"Yes, you've made that more than abundantly clear."

"And you know I need this girl, not only for the alliance but also to marry Peter and continue the Romanov line," I persist.

When he finally speaks, his voice holds bone-deep weariness.

"Of course you do. Because it never ends, does it? The politics, the manipulations. You take what you need and damn anything or anyone who gets in your way. You don't care if Peter is happy—just as long as he produces a male heir. You don't care if this girl wants to be queen—you'll put that on her just because it suits your purposes. Again and again, you'll play God, and for what? You wanted the throne. Then, once you had it, even that wasn't enough. You'll never be satisfied—never be able to find any joy in your life—because you are always burning a path toward the next trophy you must obtain."

"How *dare* you?" I practically scream. "Everything I have ever done is to protect the people I love and the nation I serve. How dare you think to sit in judgment of me?"

"I'm not judging you, though Lord knows I could. Tell me honestly, *Empress*, are you happy? Or are you haunted and buried beneath the burden of your name? Because that's the life you're about to force on this girl, Elizabeth. You made your own choice, but you are not giving her one. She's a pawn. You'll make her a queen and a Romanov, but at what cost to her? Or do you even care anymore?"

"What I care about is my family, my legacy, and my country. As for the girl, either she will carry the burden, or she will be crushed by it. That is what she must decide. So if you genuinely want to protect your poor little bird, you'd best prepare her for the weight of the crown. Because it's coming whether she likes it or not."

Sergei stands so abruptly, his chair tips over behind him, hitting the ground with a hollow thud.

"As you wish, Empress. But the girl has a name, you know. It's Sophie."

He strides out, slamming the door behind him. Only in his absence can I breathe again.

I curse loudly, pushing the inkwell from my desk and sending it splattering to the floor.

Damn it, this girl is going to be trouble.

And that, I cannot have.

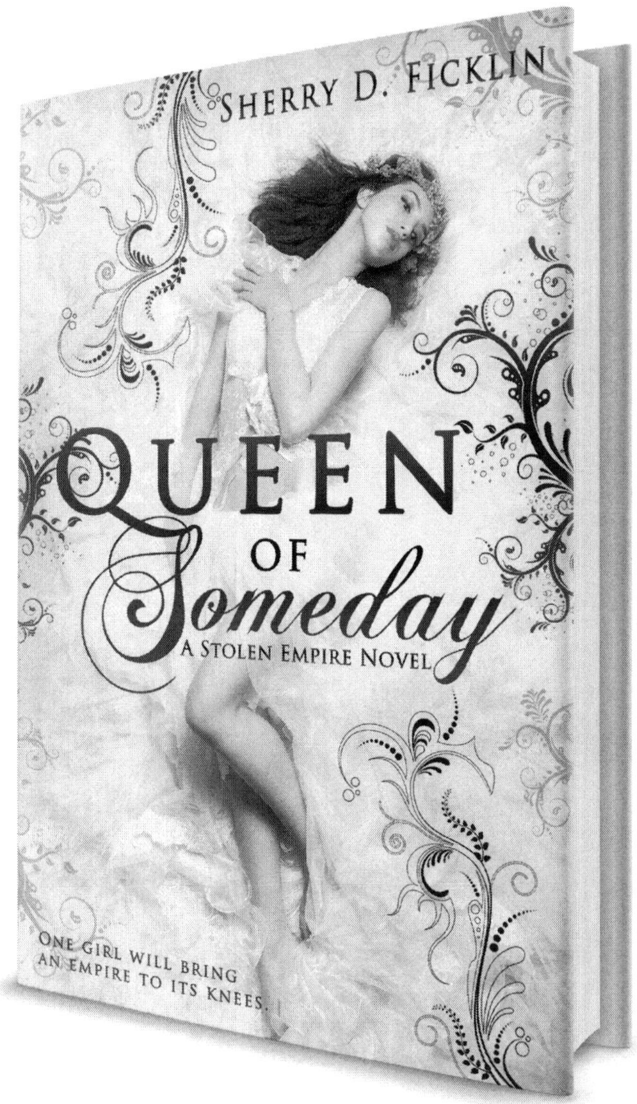

SHERRY D. FICKLIN
QUEEN
OF
Someday
A STOLEN EMPIRE NOVEL
ONE GIRL WILL BRING
AN EMPIRE TO ITS KNEES.

Prologue

And then he does the most dangerous, reckless thing he ever could have done.

He kisses me.

The moment our lips touch, the last fraying strands of my self-control snap and I reach up, clasping my hands behind his neck and pulling him against me. There's no reason, no judgment—only gentle waves of relief. I'm lost in the ocean of his embrace, drowning in him. I could live a hundred lifetimes inside his kiss, and it would never be enough. One single thought surfaces through the tide of emotions.

"Of the entire universe, I only wanted you," I whisper the words against his lips, a solemn pledge.

His hands slide up my back and into my hair, working it loose with his fingers until it falls in brown waves across my shoulders. I sigh against his mouth and he responds by pulling away just a bit, laying a kiss on the tip of my nose, my forehead, and beside my eye, before returning to my lips.

"You have ruined me," he whispers against my mouth, his voice thick with desire.

Chapter One

The sled is cramped; my legs and back ache in protest as we cut through the deep snow. I pull back the heavy damask curtain covering the small window. Outside the landscape is barren and desolate. Nothing but stark white snow for miles, interrupted by the occasional leafless tree. Though the horses race forward across the plain as fast as they are able, the trek has been long and the snow deep so they snort with exertion. We'd had to abandon our more spacious carriage in Livonia and continue the rest of the way in this small sled. Across from me, my mother carefully stitches on her small linen even as each bump threatens to destroy the colorful tapestry she's creating. She hasn't spoken to me in two days, not since I'd finally grown weary of her constant chatter about how different and lavish life would be at a *real* court and reprimanded her harshly.

I sigh deeply. Perhaps the rolling hills of Anhault-Zerbst are not as grand as the palaces of Berlin, where she grew up in the home of our wealthiest aunt, but it was my father's land and my only home. Never have I missed it more than I do on this journey, the dangerous trek through the depths of Russia in the coldest months of winter. I have acquired a constant shiver and my toes and fingers never seem to thaw. Still, it was only Mother's callous remarks about my father that had provoked me to speak rudely to her, and she is making me pay for it now, making the already cold interior of the carriage seem absolutely frigid with her indifference.

Letting the heavy damask curtain fall back into place, I sit back, stretching beneath the thick, fur blanket heaped over my legs. Closing my eyes, I rest against the seat, and I can almost feel the warm summer sun on my face. Days of running through the field with my darling little brother and sister, as we chased down chickens that had escaped the coop, float through my mind like soap bubbles. I remember sitting on the edge of the creek for hours, slipping off my shoes, letting my toes soak in the water. And sometimes Gretchen, my good friend, would come and bring flowers to weave into my dark hair or a flask of wine from her father's stock for us to drink until our heads were light as a feather. It never mattered much to me that she was the daughter of the local innkeeper and I was the daughter of the prince. We were innocent of such things, much to my mother's chagrin. I can't help but smile at the memories. As they come, I try to hold them close, weaving them around me like the fragile threads under my mother's fingers.

Such happier times, though not so long ago, seem to me now as if they occurred in another lifetime.

Everything changed when I turned fourteen. Though still a girl by any accounts, Mother was desperate to see me wed. I didn't learn until much later of our family's dire financial situation, or that Father was in danger of forfeiting his family properties.

She had first tried to wed me to young Peter, then heir to the Swiss throne. But when he abdicated to move to Russia with his aunt, all hope of that union seemed lost. Mother had been forced to offer me to my uncle, an old man with missing teeth and thin, white hair. He'd come for a visit that summer and while I had thought it an innocent visit, his intentions toward me became painfully obvious. I can still remember the stench of brandy and tobacco on his breath as he'd cornered me one evening and forced a kiss upon me.

It had taken all my will not to retch on his golden slippers.

I cried into my pillow all night when Mother told me he asked for my hand in marriage. I screamed, raged, and begged— something that did not bode well in her eyes. When the letter arrived from Empress Elizabeth of Russia, we had both been deeply relieved to say the least. I cling to that feeling now, as we trek across the tundra, snow falling all around us.

Finally, after what feels like hours, I sit forward. I'm so desperate for conversation that I ask the only question that I think might appeal to my stoic mother.

"Mother, tell me, how long do you think we are to remain at the Winter Palace?"

Her eyes flicker up to me, sparkling. She is beautiful, for all her flaws of character. Her hair is brown like mine, and perfectly smooth. Her skin is a pale crème like fresh milk, and her eyes are wide and dark blue like a storm at sea. There is absolutely nothing that makes her happier than planning what, in her mind, will be a fine royal union, and that happiness makes her even lovelier. As she answers, I would swear she is actually glowing.

"If I have my way, you will never step foot on Prussian soil again," she answers confidently. "Empress Consort," she muses wistfully, "just as I should have been."

I wish I could share her enthusiasm. Gretchen's warm smile and twinkling laugh invade my thoughts once more, and I have to force them away. It won't do to dwell on those childhood memories now. Not when my mother has made my options very clear.

"It's not an engagement," I say softly. "Not

officially."

Empress Elizabeth's letter had been vague at best. A simple invitation for my mother and me to join her at Russian Court. There was not even a hint of what my mother longed for so desperately—a marriage between myself and Peter, once heir to Sweden and now the future King of Russia. Still, Mother packed us up immediately and we made for St. Petersburg even through the blistering winter, hoping to make our arrival by Peter's sixteenth birthday.

"Not yet, perhaps. But the empress favors our family—my family, that is—and she knows the best way to secure her throne is by securing her bloodline. And for that, she needs not only Peter as heir, but for Peter himself to have an heir. And for that, she will need you."

Or another princess. I don't say the words, but they buzz in my head like honeybees. The prince's birthday celebration is sure to be filled with eligible ladies from every corner of the kingdom, each vying for a place beside him. I myself have met Peter only once, when we were ten years old. He was bratty and insufferable as all boys are, but even at that age, he had subtle nobility about him, a tilt of the chin, and a confidence in his gait that only royals possess.

Deep in the back of my mind, I couldn't help but wonder what sort of man Peter had become. Is he kind? Handsome? Strong? Wise? In my mind, I allow a vague image of him to form. Surely, he would be handsome, as were the other men in his family. And even in the remote area of my home, word of his skill in the hunt and his predilection for archery were well known. Certainly, he will be a good husband and a fair and just king.

While I daydream, Mother begins to drone on about the lavish balls that we will attend, and the frivolous and silly-sounding customs I will be expected to learn to fit in at Royal Court. I lay my head back gently as she speaks, the sound of her voice soothing after such a long silence. The sled bucks and I fly forward into her lap, spilling the contents of her sewing basket.

"What in the world?" she demands as I right myself. "Why have we stopped?"

I draw back the curtain and our escort, General Pitankin, rides past the window, his chestnut mare jerking the reins skittishly.

"Stay inside," he commands.

My mother grabs a dainty, blue fan from the seat beside her and begins fanning herself despite the cold.

"I'm sure it's just beggars. I believe these woods are filled with them," she offers as if to console me.

Outside, the general yells something in Russian. I curse myself mentally. If only I had thought to learn Russian along with French and German, I wouldn't feel quite so foreign now. Still, if Mother is successful in her ambitions, I will learn the language soon enough.

There are sounds of a scuffle, and the unmistakable ring of a steel blade being drawn from its sheath. The sled rocks sideways as someone knocks into it. Mother lets out a startled squeal. I lean forward, peeking out the curtain, and see the general and another of our guards on the ground, unmoving. Quickly, I lift the hem of my brown, wool gown and slip a knife from my boot. Mother opens her mouth, I'm sure to chastise me for such an unladylike thing as having a knife hidden on my person, but I silence her with a finger to my lips. While my mother had been determined to groom me to be a proper lady, my father was content to let me join him in hunting, fencing, and even knife throwing. The small blade in my hand is one of many he's gifted me over the years, and the hilt is warm and comforting in my palm.

The sled rocks again, and I hear the stomp of boots as the thieves begin pulling our trunks from the back. They won't find any riches, only recently altered dresses and sturdy undergarments we've brought with us. Any jewels Mother might have brought are most likely hidden down the front of her corset—and there would be few of those at that. Despite being the ruler of our province, my father has no kingly riches. Our wealth lies in our title alone—a fact Mother never allows him to forget.

Soon, they are muttering in disappointed tones.

I know they will come for us next; there is nothing left for them now but to amuse themselves with us. Nodding to Mother, who looks like she's about to faint, I quietly slip out of the opposite side of the sled and slink around its wooden bow, knife in hand. Snow crunches beneath my boots, but the restless stomping of the horses obscures it. I know I'm no match for them on fair terms, but if I can surprise them, then we have a chance of escape.

I see two pairs of legs standing beside the sled. Then I hear the door fly open, and my mother screams. Lunging forward, I slice into the first thief's thigh, high up where I know the blood will flow too quickly to stop. The knife is sharp enough that it takes him a moment to realize what's happening. Climbing to my feet, I lunge at the next man, who is much quicker than I hoped, and he waves off my attack. I spin, a move I've practiced more than once with the butcher's children when we used to play wooden swords, and crouch below his grasp, slicing a line through his gut. The smell is thick and sour as his innards spill out, sloshing to the ground as he falls. I gag, and bile rises in my throat. My eyes water immediately, and it's all I can do not to collapse to my knees.

I'm so busy trying to get myself together that I don't see the third man coming. Before I can think to fight him off, two strong arms coil around me as my mother continues to scream. He squeezes, and

I can't breathe. The knife falls from my hand as I thrash wildly. He's yelling at me in his foreign tongue, but I can't even draw breath to tell him that I don't understand. Just as my vision begins to explode with light, I manage to kick the side of the carriage hard enough to topple us both into the new-fallen snow. He falls flat to his back, and I crash on top of him. I hear the air violently rush form his lungs, and he releases me. Rolling to my feet, I scoop up the knife and run as fast as my numb feet will carry me.

The woods are thick and blanketed with snow. I'm light enough that I don't sink too deep as I fly through the forest, but behind me, I hear the crunch of the snow as my attacker pursues, each step slow and labored.

Good. Let him chase me. I can get him away from my mother, then, hopefully, double back and grab her. We will unhitch the sled, and she and I can ride on to St. Petersburg with just the horses. The sky is grey and the air frigid in my lungs. Each breath burns, and then expels in a ball of steam out of my mouth. Still, I run. Turning to spare a glance over my shoulder unbalances me and I fall, slipping down the slope of a hill, tumbling into a deep snow bank. I lay there for a moment, trying to catch my breath and staring at the sky above me, and I listen for his footsteps.

There's nothing.

Rolling onto my side, I peek up. The snow is

deep, well over my knees, and I struggle to get back to solid ground. A patch of pine trees offers respite. The snow around them is shallow, and I take a minute to brush the ice from my hair. It has fallen free from its elegant braid and dangles in wet clumps around my face. Still, I have somehow managed to hold onto the knife.

In the distance, I hear a gunshot. The sound echoes through the bleak forest like cannon fire. I turn without hesitation and run back toward my mother, cursing my stupidity. What had I been thinking leaving her alone like that? The bandit must have doubled back to her, thinking me long gone. As I make my way up the steep hill, I slip and fall to my knees in something slimy and wet. It isn't snow but mud, a small spring of warm water bubbling up from the ground. Somehow, the snow had hidden it from my sight, but now, it's all down the front of me. The water and mud pulls down on my already-ruined gown, as if trying to hold me to the earth. I frown at the sight. Poor Mother. She'd paid the seamstress what little money we had to refashion this dress for me. It had been one of her old walking gowns but the seamstress had added lace and a beautiful yellow sash, all of which was now covered in muck. With haste, I untie the sash and slip the bulky gown over my head. The chill is immediate, but still, I feel lighter, light enough to run once more. I run my hands over my corset and decide to rid myself of it while I'm at it. Using the knife, I quickly cut the strings and discard it. Not only can I take a real breath, but also my petticoat is clean and white as snow, helping me blend in. Scrambling back to my feet, I press forward. As soon as I appear over the ridge, I see a man standing at the edge of the cliff not five feet to my left. He looks over, his eyes locking with mine.

He doesn't look like a bandit, I realize. He wears a long, black brocade jacket with golden embroidery; a black, fur hat stuffed on his head makes his blue eyes glow like azure. He's clean, calm, and holding a rife—which is pointed at me for only a moment before he lowers it, a confused expression on his face. I hold out my tiny blade in front of me, as if it would do any good. He cocks his head to the side curiously before addressing me in perfect German.

"Princess Sophia? I'm Sergei Salkov of Her Majesty's Imperial Court. I'm here to rescue you."

Just as the words leave his mouth, something moves in the corner of my eye. The bandit who has been chasing me rushes forward from behind a thick tree, right toward Sergei. The tall, scruffy man is draped in heavy furs and even at full speed, he's moving too slowly to cross the distance between them before I turn the knife in my hand and throw it. It lands with a dull thud in the center of his chest. He swears loudly and then falls forward, the snow around him turning to crimson slush.

As gently as possible, I wrap my arms around my waist and hug myself, rubbing the exposed skin to stave off the frigid cold. I glance up and see Sergei has his rifle lowered at the ground and is staring at the now-fallen bandit. Then he's looks back at me with his mouth twisted into a funny grin.

Not sure what the protocol is for meeting a stranger in my undergarments, I dip into a formal curtsy. "It is a pleasure to meet you, sir, but I think perhaps you are a bit late for that."

Chapter Two

The sound my mother makes when I step back into sight near the road is somewhere between relief and exasperation. Beside her, two royal guards are trying to reload the toppled trunks of gowns, but she turns and orders them to stop. I look over and see that each dress, so carefully refitted and repurposed, has been shredded. Surely, the bandits didn't do such a thing?

"Leave them. They have been utterly destroyed." She turns to me, wearing an expression of shock and indignation, "Can you imagine? Bandits? What a dreadful thing. Thank heavens Her Majesty thought to send us a royal escort or we would both be dead!"

Her face flushes as her voice raises pitch. No doubt, she is thinking even now how this tragedy might be used to her advantage. Her head snaps back to me, as if she's really looking at me for the first time.

"My heavens, Sophie! Where are your clothes? Did that horrible man…?" She doesn't finish the sentence. I know where her mind is spinning off to. If he had touched me in any way, I would be ruined. Sullied and unfit to marry the prince.

"No, Mother. I only fell in some thick mud. I had to rid myself of the gown in order to escape."

She lowers her chin and appraises me carefully, as if she could see the damaged virtue like a spot on her favorite table linen. Finally, she nods, accepting me at my word. Beside me, Sergei slips off his coat and drapes it over my shoulders. It's warm and soft and smells vaguely like the winter pine of my homeland.

"Here you go, Princess. You must have a terrible chill. Would you like us to make a fire for you to warm yourself before we continue to the palace?"

His voice is tender, the way a person might speak to a child. I'm not sure why, but it unsettles me. Perhaps it is pride, but I don't like it at all.

"I'm quite all right, I assure you. I think my mother would be quite pleased to ride on ahead. No need to make a fuss." I pause. "And please, call me Sophie."

He bows his head. "As you wish, Sophie."

He barks orders to his men, who form a tight ring around the carriage with their horses.

"Are you quite certain those bandits won't come back?" Mother asks as she hikes up her skirts and climbs back into the sled.

Sergei smiles, winking at me behind her back. I

catch his eye, and a small warmth forms in my belly.

"I'm quite sure they are gone. And should we be set upon again, I'm sure young Sophie will defend your honor."

I can't help but grin at his words. I carefully climb in behind Mother, and Sergei follows me.

"In any case, I shall ride here with you—for your protection, of course."

Mother shrugs indifferently, and Sergei takes a seat beside me.

"They destroyed all our lovely gowns," Mother begins, not meeting his eyes. "We will need new ones. And since this attack occurred on Her Majesty's road—"

Sergei waves her off as if it's nothing. "Yes, of course. I will let the empress know the situation. I'm sure she will make recompense."

Mother nods and sits back, closing her eyes as the carriage rolls into motion.

Sergei leans over to me, his voice a whisper.

"Where did you learn to handle a knife like that?"

Mother answers, her eyes still closed, but her nose wrinkling up in disgust as she speaks.

"Her father let the child run quite wild during our time in Settin. Too indulgent, I always told him so. Young ladies should be taught to sing and sew, not to fight and swing a sword. Still, dangerous times he would say. Posh. To this day, the girl can't sew a straight line and her singing voice is just awful." As if suddenly aware she was articulating all the wrong things to a man who, for all she knew, had the ear of the empress, she sits up starkly, opening her eyes. "That is, Princess Sophia's strength lies in other accomplishments. She can play the piano quite well, she can read Latin, and she is in every way a true Lady of Prussia."

"I quite agree," Sergei says gently. Mother nods and rests back again. Within minutes, she's snoring gently.

Even under the warmth of his coat, I'm shivering. I hope Sergei doesn't notice the uncontrollable shaking as we bounce along. After a few minutes, he takes my hands in his. I open my mouth to protest, but he brings my fingers to his mouth and blows on them. The warmth of his breath feels so good against my frozen skin that I almost sigh in relief. He repeats the process a few times, blowing my hands and then rubbing them with his. All the while, I'm watching his face. It's not a romantic gesture, yet it's strangely intimate. I don't think I've ever been touched like this before, not by a man—and a terribly handsome man at that. My heart races in my chest, making me warm with flush.

"Better?" he asks finally.

I nod, taking my hands back reluctantly and folding them in my lap. "Yes. Thank you."

He grins. "So, tell me about yourself, Princess."

The muscles in my back stiffen. I wait for a

moment, half expecting my mother to jump in with some nonsense about my feminine skills, most of which are blatantly untrue.

"I like to ride," I say weakly.

"Do you hunt?" he asks.

I nod. "I'm a good shot too."

A strange lump forms in my throat, as I realize I may never hunt with my father again.

"Good," Sergei says cryptically, peeking his head out of the carriage window.

"Does that happen often? The attack, I mean. Do you often have a problem with bandits on the road?"

He sits back, looking at me thoughtfully before answering.

"No, never."

"Then why did the empress send you to escort us?" I ask.

He's quiet, looking lost in thought. "The empress didn't send me."

I watch as an array of emotions play out across his chiseled face, worry, dread, and finally, resignation. He says nothing else, but I can read the tension in his squared shoulders, the tick working in his jaw.

"It wasn't a random attack, was it?" I ask boldly. "It was an assassination attempt."

His eyes flicker to mine. "You are a surprising creature, Princess. Clever as well as brave. Wherever did you come from?"

I ignore the backhanded compliment.

"Why would someone attack us?"

He frowns, wiping his hand down his face and rubbing his neck.

"There are those in court who are unhappy at the prospect of an alliance between Prussia and Russia, those who seek instead to fortify a bond with Austria. The empress favors you and your family, but that favor will extend only so far. If they can prove you unfit—in any way—she will have no choice but to send you away and find an Austrian princess to put on the throne."

I take a deep breath, drawing myself up in my seat.

"Then I must be sure they have no complaint against me. Thank you for your honesty. I appreciate your warnings, and I will heed them." I pause before adding, "And thank you for riding out to save us."

Reaching up, he picks a small clump of mud from my hair.

"Oh, I suspect you had the situation well in hand."

I drift in and out of sleep as we ride on through the day. Just as dusk falls, Sergei nudges me gently.

"We have arrived, Princess."

Pushing back the curtain, I watch out the window as we roll into the grand city of St.

Petersburg. Even in the dim glow of the setting sun, the view is breathtaking. The iron-and-gold gates of the Winter Palace stretch before us, the Romanov crest, a glorious golden crowned eagle, watching us from the top. The carriage stops and Sergei steps out, speaking to the guards in quick Russian. The gates slide open and we roll inside, Sergei waving to me as we pass. The grounds are a menagerie of ice sculptures and glowing lanterns. I expect the carriage to stop in front of the grand entrance but it continues, rounding to the rear of the massive estate. Two guards step forward to assist us out as Sergei reappears and leads us into the servants' entrance.

"Why on earth were we not greeted formally?" Mother demands as we weave through the empty kitchens. The hearth is roaring with fire, and I can feel the chill melting out of my skin.

"Surely you would not have the young princess introduced to court in just her petticoats?" Sergei says in the tone one might use with a whining child.

She sighs. "No, of course not."

He tilts his head in a gesture of deference and leads on, up the back staircase and down the left wing of a long, ornate hallway. The walls are marble and granite with decorative, golden wreaths and swirling vines along the ceiling. Massive frescos and beautifully woven tapestries hang from the walls, while tables with fresh-cut flowers sit at every door. I'm tempted to remark on the absurdity of it—fresh flowers in the middle of winter. Being raised by a man who saw such things as unnecessary frivolities, it's an instant reaction. But I'm sure here, at the Grand Imperial Court, they don't have an old man hunched over a ledger complaining about the cost of tulips, so I bite my tongue. I must remember that here, excess is completely ordinary and I ought not to make a fuss about it.

"These are your rooms," he says motioning to the last door at the end of the hall. The steward pushes the massive, oak door open, and the sitting room inside is nearly the size of my entire home back in Settin. There's a writing desk, piano, and half a dozen chairs and chaises scattered about. A large, round table boasts a silver tray full of meats, cheeses, and breads. There are three doors beyond, two seem to be bedchambers, but I'm not sure about the third. I'm quite sure these rooms alone are the size of our entire home back in Germany. I look to Mother, who frowns, unimpressed.

"Are the accommodations to your liking?" Sergei asks me directly, as Mother begins touring the room, commenting on the color of the drapes and the size of the fireplace.

I nod. "They are; thank you."

"Then I will leave you to rest. I will send up a maid with some nightclothes, and I will have the seamstress attend you first thing in the morning."

Mother turns, "Do tell the empress we've arrived.

I'm sure she will be most excited to see me."

Sergei bows gallantly. His eyes flicker up for only a moment and catch mine. A sly grin spreads across his face as he stands and turns to leave, the white-wigged steward closing the door behind them. No sooner are they gone than Mother opens the third door and nods happily.

"A washroom. Good. I could use a hot bath after such a strenuous journey." She turns to look at me. I hold up the hem of my soiled petticoat. She frowns. "You will need to wash too, of course. But I should go first. You will spoil the water with your muck."

Opening our door, she orders the steward back, demanding hot water be brought up from the kitchens.

Sometime later, the water has grown cool as I finally slip out of my clothes and into the tub. Still, it's warm on my cold skin. The soap smells like honey and goats milk as I wash away the last of the snow and mud from my body and hair. I rest back against the side of the copper washtub and try to imagine in my head what it might be like to see Peter again. He would have grown devastatingly handsome, that much I can be sure of, and he will see me and smile. He will take my hand, we will dance and laugh, and he will insist we go for a walk in the garden. The moonlight will be pale and glowing, he will look into my eyes, and… I let the vision trail off. For a moment, one insane second, it wasn't Peter, but

Sergei's face in my thoughts. I brush it aside quickly. Sergei is a kind man, handsome, and not much older than I am. A gentleman who went out of his way to keep me safe. But even so, he is not the reason I'm here, and I cannot afford to be distracted by a few kind words and handsome eyes.

I must win the heart of the future king.

"Come along, dear. As I expected, we have been summoned to see the empress first thing in the morning. You will need to be rested."

With a heavy sigh, I step out of the bath and dry myself before slipping into the soft, green dressing gown the maid brought for me.

When I walk into the room, Mother is sitting at the writing desk, furiously scribbling notes on parchment.

"Are you writing Father? To let him know we arrived safely?" I ask.

She looks up at me and blinks, as if the idea was so foreign that it never crossed her mind.

"Of course not. I'm writing to King Fredrick."

"Oh," I say flatly.

King Fredrick of Germany had been overjoyed at the prospect of my sitting on the throne when we stopped for a visit in Berlin on our way here. He sees it as a way to secure an alliance, Mother sees it as a way to regain her lifestyle, and I see it as the only alternative to marrying my Uncle Edward.

She points the feather quill at me. "Make no

mistake, Sophia, this union is a political alliance sanctioned by the king himself. And if you are successful in securing the prince's hand in marriage, our family will be rewarded with wealth enough to rival the most prestigious noble's in Berlin."

I freeze. The thought of facing this task alone is beyond daunting. Dread shoots up my back like spikes.

"Will you go back then? Back to Prussia?"

She pauses, then sets down the pen and holds her hands out to me. I step forward and take them. "Sweet child. I will never leave you. For as long as you need me by your side, I will remain. Even if it means living with these monstrous Russian winters."

I smile, relief flooding through me. Mother might be shallow and, at times, callous, but what she does, she does for me and for our family. It's easy to forget that sometimes.

She sends me off to bed; the warm blankets and soft pillows soothe me into an instant slumber. All too soon, I see the first rays of daylight sneaking through the slit in the curtains. The maid from last night rushes in and throws them open, flooding the room with warmth and light. I sit up, rubbing my eyes.

"Thank you," I mutter. "I'm sorry; I've forgotten your name."

The maid curtsies. "Isobel, my lady."

"Thank you, Isobel. Is the seamstress here yet?"

"She only just arrived."

"Thank you," I say, throwing back the blankets. Isobel gathers them and begins making the bed as I step out into the foyer.

There are three trunks of gowns, all open and overflowing as Mother and the seamstress bicker. As soon as I enter, the seamstress bows her neck.

"My lady."

I nod. "What is all this?"

"Fifteen gowns," Mother says, throwing her hands in the air dramatically. "You are getting fifteen new gowns."

I step forward. "That's wonderful."

Mother snorts in disagreement. "No, it's barely enough to replace what we lost. And I am only getting nine."

I don't remind her that we only had four gowns between us, and that they were mysteriously destroyed. Or that all four were old and had been remade at least half a dozen times already.

Instead, I turn to the seamstress. "The empress is too generous. We are grateful."

The seamstress smiles and motions for me to come to her. She appraises me thoughtfully.

"You are about the size of my daughter, lucky enough. She often stands for me to try new fabrics and styles on. And your coloring, the brown hair and dark blue eyes, you will look lovely in most colors. I'm so glad. Only last week we had to work for a lady with hair orange as fire and pale skin. There were so few colors we could put her in that didn't make her look sick."

She prattles on under the watchful eye of my mother as she discusses patterns, bustle sizes, and sashes. I just close my eyes, lift my arms when told to, and let them choose. There's a sharp tap at the door and the steward comes in, a large box in his arms. He sets it on the floor and backs up.

"A gift from Lord Salkov."

Mother shoos the steward out and opens the box, pulling out a lovely pink-and-black lace gown. The style is French, a low bodice and tight sleeves. Compared to anything else I've ever had, it's downright scandalous. Yet, I remember seeing many ladies dressed in similar styles in Berlin and the idea of wearing it, looking so grown up, makes my heart pound. The notion of Sergei admiring me in it makes my heart pound harder.

Mother holds it up to herself and grins wildly. "It's just lovely. I think I'll go put it on."

"Don't be silly. It's for the princess. See the cut of the waist? It's far too narrow for you," the seamstress says, not looking up from her work.

Frowning, Mother drapes the gown over her arm. "Insolent girl. The gown is obviously for me."

I shrug, "Maybe he's put a note in the box?"

Mother walks to the box and pulls a tiny scrap of paper out, reading it aloud.

"'Since you have no gown to wear today, please accept this humble gift.' It's signed Sergei Salkov. It doesn't say who it's for."

I point to her bedchamber. "You have the gown you were wearing yesterday. I have no gown at all," I say simply.

She glares at me. "I can't wear that. It's filthy."

The seamstress looks up at me with sympathy in her eyes.

"Well, then I suppose I will have to meet the empress naked. I'm sure she will understand, Mother. I mean, it wouldn't make her think less of me—of my fitness to marry her nephew—to meet her like this, don't you think? Yes, I'm sure she will understand."

I hold my breath. I've never employed this particular tactic with her before, and I'm not sure how she will react. I've put her vanity against her plotting as I've seen my father do so many times. It's always a risk. Sometimes, she would react with a quiet acceptance of his will. Other times, she simply tightened her mouth into a line and left, scheming behind his back until she achieved her goals.

She stares at me for a second before tossing the gown on the seat beside me.

"You are quite right, of course. A kind gift though it is, I will simply have to let you borrow it for the day. I'm sure Sergei will understand."

And with that, she spins on her heel and heads

into her bedchamber, closing the door behind her. On her knees in front of me, the seamstress smiles widely and winks at me.

The maid is helping me into my gown when the steward arrives with a request from the empress to join her for breakfast in her private chambers. Mother, dressed and leaving her room for the first time since her tantrum, accepts the invitation graciously and helps Isobel finish buttoning the dress. Behind me, Mother drapes something across my neck. Catching a glimpse of it in the mirror as she fastens the clasp, I gasp softly. It's one of the few jewels her family passed down to her, and one of her prized possessions. A dozen black-onyx teardrops dangle from a strand of black beads at the base of my neck. The stones are warm against my skin and I wonder if she's been holding them all this time, debating whether to put them on me or wear them herself. Apparently, her desire to put me on the throne is greater than her own vanity—which is something I won't soon forget.

After all, Johanna of Holsein-Gottorp was born a princess, the great-granddaughter of the King of Denmark, but after being forced to marry a man beneath her rank, she lost nearly everything. The jewels were all she had, the last link to the bright future that had—in her mind—been stolen from her. Now, with an opportunity to set me on a throne, she hopes to reclaim a little bit of that future. I'm not about to complain. Not when, until the empress' invitation arrived, she had been content to marry me off to the highest bidder, no matter how wretched the prospects might be.

And I have no doubt that if I fail in this endeavor, that is exactly the fate that I will return home to.

With that in mind, I straighten myself up, smooth my bustle, and raise my chin. Mother twists my hair into a lovely, but simple roll across my forehead and secures it with a pin. Finally ready, we follow the steward out of the room ant toward the empress' chambers.

AUTHORS NOTE

And now, my dear readers, we have come full circle in this saga. I do hope you've enjoyed taking this journey with me, because I have loved every single moment of it. As always, I have changed names and dates, though the bulk of the story presented is historically accurate. It always fascinated me how two women could be so similar and so vastly different. It reminds me that no matter where we begin, we are all the masters of our own fate, and every choice we make writes our story for us. When writing a book, I always finish the end first, so I know where I am heading. And life gives us the same opportunity. We begin with an idea of our end goal and do our best to work toward it, hoping we can stay on the path that will lead us there. Though in life, as with writing, there are always bumps along the way, and we sometimes find ourselves far from the path we thought we'd take. But, as long as we have our goal in mind, we can always reach it.

So go, my wonderful readers, and write your own story.

Acknowledgements

This series has been a wonderful and unexpected journey. It was achieved only by the grace of a dedicated group of people without whom, these words would still be living only inside my head.

To the wonderful team at CTP, who have been my champions as I told the story I wanted, in the way I wanted, despite what others tried to make it. You ladies have been nothing short of a godsend and I am deeply grateful you ever took a chance on me.

To my longsuffering family, who has been there through all the ups and downs, the elated highs and the depressing lows that make up so much of the business of being a writer, thank you for all the love, support, and tolerance as I made this journey.

To my behind the scenes team of rock stars, June Westerfield, Ethan Gregory, and Stephenee Carsten. You three are my guiding stars, and nothing in my world works without you. You are truly the best friends a girl could ask for.

For Jon Messenger and Julie Wetzel, who are fabulous authors in their own right and also the best convention family a girl could ask for. Thanks for slugging it out with me in the cheap seats. Here's hoping we have many more adventures together.

And to my amazing street team and loyal readers: YOU make all this possible—and worth every struggle. I can not express my love and gratitude for each of you.

Thank you!

About the Author

Sherry Ficklin is the author of over a dozen novels including the bestselling Stolen Empire series. When she's not busy writing, she is usually found tinkering on her alpaca farm or speaking at writing conventions. You can see more about her work on her official website, **www.sherryficklin.com** or stalk her on Facebook or Instagram **@sherry_ficklin.**